FINDING ASHER

Book II of the Search and Rescue Dog Series

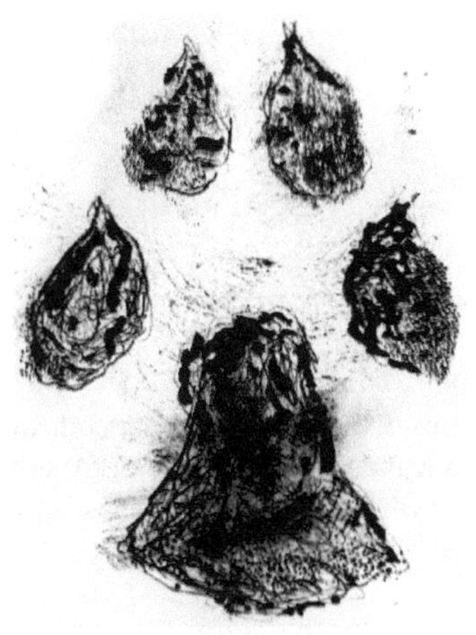

SCOTT HAMMOND

Black Rose Writing | Texas

ISBN: 978-1-68513-308-5
PUBLISHED BY BLACK ROSE WRITING
www.blackrosewriting.com

Printed in the United States of America
Suggested Retail Price (SRP) $17.95

Finding Asher is printed in Minion Pro

*As a planet-friendly publisher, Black Rose Writing does its best to eliminate unnecessary waste to reduce paper usage and energy costs, while never compromising the reading experience. As a result, the final word count vs. page count may not meet common expectations.

FINDING ASHER

PART I
UP THE MOUNTAIN

CHAPTER 1

Frozen muscles. Hollow stare. Blank face. He stood over the body. The music in Asher's head was gone. No melody. No rhyme or chorus. For the first time ever, the repeating song that piloted his life was gone. Now, just silence. He stood alone with himself, in a giant void of meaning.

Then, brick by brick, the wall cracked, and the sounds of the outer world trickled in. First, Asher heard the unseen bugs and birds that, in the sizzling heat of the summer day, were the background noises of the foothill forest. He felt a dry, cooling breeze and heard the rattling of brown leaves. Finally, the distant sound of water over rocks reached his awakening ears. Then the splashing of a waterfall. He had no feelings for these sounds. They were the reorienting ticking sounds that let him reenter the paused world.

Asher looked directly into his father's vacant expression. He was facing the sky with his head on a small log and his body in the grass paralleling the trail. It was not an obvious and dramatic death, just a quiet snuffing of the light.

Without visible emotion, Asher reached across his father's stilled chest and took the hiking pole out of the hollow shell's hand. He slipped the strap off the wrist, touching the pale cold skin. He pulled the pole into his arms and held it to his chest for a moment.

Just an hour ago, his father had awkwardly held Asher to his chest, something he almost never did. He'd looked into Asher's confused eyes and whispered things he'd needed to say, but would never be understood. That had been his father's last chance to tell his autistic son how much Asher had blessed his life. Tell him his unique brain had awoken the love he did not know he had. Tell him Asher was the blessing that saved his marriage. The words and spontaneous affection had confused Asher. The firehose of emotion had passed right through him.

Holding the third hiking pole, Asher oriented. He replayed his recent memory back to find his familiar routine. Back to the car, the parking lot, and the steady beat of footfalls on the trail. He replayed in his near perfect memory the melody of his father's comforting voice, talking, sometimes singing as they hiked up the trail. They were on the trail together, headed to a clear and familiar destination, to the lake, to the camp, with a campfire, tent, sleeping bag and visor. On this trip, they had left at the same time they always did, and followed the same path with the same routine to the same destination. Carefully, they had packed the same provisions in the same place in his backpack. But on this day, the comfort of routine was shattered when his forever hiking companion coughed, awkwardly took off his pack, grabbed his left arm, then his chest, and fell.

Father lay on the ground, sometimes thrashing his legs and moaning, while Asher watched in the shade of a tree, waiting for him to get over his ailment. Asher had seen such episodes in an institutional care center when he was a boy, before he had been introduced to his father and mother. Patients gasping, grasping, flailing, and lost. But that was long ago. Twenty years ago. He had never seen father like this. His father, who had come into his life later, when he was six, and who had become his life's rhythm and melody.

After his father's burst of words and emotions, Asher backed off. Away. Trying to make sense. He looked over to see his father's outreached arm and moved closer, wanting to hear but not touch. His father's tangled words that sounded like an orchestra tuning up, waiting for Asher to touch him. Knowing there would be no reciprocity, and hoping there would be no resistance, the dying man awkwardly grabbed Asher around his neck and pulled himself to Asher's ear. "Go," he stammered slowly.

Asher gave his father no comfort. He did not know how. He just stared with an expressionless face as his father strained and then went limp. Asher watched as his face relaxed. His eyes were empty. When the music and rhythm stopped, the brick wall of silence came.

Asher stood in the grass by the trail, leaning on his hiking poles, trying to make sense of what had just happened. Overwhelmed in a fog of surprise, the only way out was to find the familiar. Find his way back to the routine. Asher took the food bag out of his father's pack. Bread, creamy peanut butter, macaroni and cheese, spaghetti and tomato sauce with no meat or vegetables, and hot chocolate with small marshmallows. Then he picked up his father's hiking pole. Asher always had two hiking poles of his own. Now he would hold one in one hand, and two in the other, and he would do what his father had said, and "go." He collected his knees and ankles under his awkward but strong, tall body. Then he slowly rose. He stuffed the food bag in his pack, and pulled it on, right strap, left strap, chest strap, waist strap. It was over forty pounds, but for Asher who carried a pack every day when he hiked with his father, it was not heavy. He was 225 lean pounds, with tree trunk legs of a timber jack body, and a round, expressionless face. To most people, from a distance, he looked normal, until they got close enough to see his eyes. Or, more accurately, see him turn his eyes away to avoid social connection.

From where he stood, Asher could see the valley below through the trees, and the peaks above him where the lake spread out in the gap between the two mountains. He looked at the hiking pole and audibly repeated his father's last word. "Go." Then he thought, *go where?* He needed to finish the hike and rendezvous with the friend. So, in his linear mind, there was only one direction to go. He stood and walked up the trail towards the lake, leaving his father's remains for others to deal with. He hoped he could get a campsite on the far side of the lake, where he could be away from other campers. Perhaps his father would join them later, his mind told him. But his heart had a different, more sinister message that he had to work hard to ignore.

After a mile of climbing, Asher heard people coming down the trail coming towards him. Someone was whistling. Then an overly friendly older couple appeared from around the corner, looking tired, but full of energy.

"Going to the lake?" the old man asked, too loud and too friendly for even normal people.

His wife brought up the rear and paused. "The last part is pretty steep," she offered her advice.

They appeared to be happy to have someone to talk at. If they had been talking to Asher, they would have seen the blank look in his eyes. Instead, they were chatting away, not waiting for a response. Still, Asher stopped in the same way his father would have. He counted to ten, stared at the trail winding through the forest, and said nothing while the strangers continued to talk. He knew if he made no eye contact and said nothing, he would not need to engage.

When he got to ten, he put his head down and continued his rapid pace, leaving the puzzled pair of senior hikers shaking their heads and saying, "Have a nice day," to the back of his head.

Farther up the trail, he stopped at a side spur. As he had always done with his father, he walked a hundred feet to a small waterfall. Keeping true to the routine his father created, he took off his pack, sat on the flat boulder just below the spray, took his boots off, and dangled his feet in the cool water. Then he reached into his backpack and took out the red bandana, and the plastic bag, to discover the predictable lunch his mother had made. The creamy peanut butter on white bread sandwiches with the crust trimmed off were precisely cut corner to corner. Asher laid them out on the plate he placed in the middle of the bandana. He placed the cup of vanilla pudding in the middle of the bandana, then carefully placed a transparent plastic spoon across the top of the pudding container.

When the meal was perfectly laid out, he ate the quarter sandwiches in order, going clockwise around the bandana. Then he picked up the pudding, pulled off and licked the lid, and dipped the clear plastic spoon into the mix. It was his favorite comfort food, and he and his father brought one container of pudding for each meal. When the pudding was gone, he placed the container in a pocket in his pack reserved for garbage, then washed off the spoon in the flowing stream.

"You'll need that for later," he said out loud, parroting his father, who was not there to say it. Then he placed his socks and boots back on his feet and looked around for his father to help tie them. Even though he was in his mid-twenties, he still could not tie his boots, so he tucked the laces into his socks. Then he took some duct tape from the repairs pocket in his pack and taped his boots on around his ankles. While doing that, he remembered his father was sick, or asleep, or maybe dead, and probably would not be coming on this trip. It was up to him to make camp and meet the visitor.

With an imprint of urgency combined with assumed responsibility, he slid off the rock, shouldered his pack, took two hiking poles in one hand and one in another, and returned to the main trail. At the junction, he turned uphill towards the mountain and began walking towards the wilderness.

CHAPTER 2

For only the third time in his young career as a sheriff deputy, Iawani Kaanapu reached for the switches and turned on both the lights and siren. He had used his lights to pull over speeders, but in this small town, where everyone knew everyone, people pulled over if his sheriff's cruiser came to a few car lengths behind them. This was a real "code." A genuine urgent emergency.

The acceleration of the older model car with the monster engine pushed his 300-pound frame into his seat. With the wig-wagging light overhead and the siren screaming, the man who called himself "Island boy" felt a rush, though he was disappointed there were only cows in the fields to see him shoot down the country road.

Iawani had grown up on "The Big Island" of Hawaii, where he had spent about half of his waking hours in the waves, coves and lava cliffs around Captain Cook Bay. His auntie, who'd had a lot to do with his upbringing, said she thought he'd been born with fish gills. In high school, he'd played rugby, and later, football. He had not planned to go to college, but a university in Utah had dangled a football scholarship in front of his nose while his parents and auntie were watching, and he could not say "no." In Utah he had other family, but he also fell in love. Not with a person, but with a geography. In his required English class, he'd read the western writer Wallace Stegner, who called the intermountain west "the geography of hope." So far from the tides of the Hawaiian Islands that many call "paradise," Iawani found his love of the land-locked, snow-capped mountains and the diverse people who called them home.

Iawani's father worked in transportation security at the Kona airport. When the big island boy had finished his college playing career, and the professionals had not come knocking, his father encouraged his athletic son to enter the police academy to become a "real cop." Someone who helped people, and not just checked to see if they had sharp objects in their carry-on luggage.

When Iawani was sworn in as a deputy in the Lincoln County Sheriff's Department in Wyoming, the sheriff was surprised that about fifty people who called themselves his cousins showed up in Lincoln. Some townspeople called it a Polynesian invasion, but the criticism died after everyone in town was invited to join the cousins for a celebration that included shrimp, a roast pig, two-dozen deep-fried chickens, and four gallons of macaroni salad. They took over the city park and cooked, ate, sang, and danced into the night to celebrate. Everyone ate leftovers for the next three days.

During the celebration, no one mentioned that a dozen big city departments had turned Iawani down. "Too big," they said. "Out of shape," even though he had passed the three-mile police academy fitness run test and was top in his class in self-defense and swimming.

He had been on the job for a year now and, in that time, he had learned where to get free donuts, and had not seen the inside of a gym, except to pick up his girlfriend. Like most new officers, he was given the oldest car, assigned to work traffic, and filled in as the resource officer at the local high school. Before long, Iawani also worked as an assistant high school football coach.

Like on the islands, most days in Lincoln County were pretty laid back. There were no gangs, and no organized crime. But people did get into trouble.

For the last five minutes, Iawani had heard the chatter, as the usual laid-back voices became precise and professional. Sally, the dispatcher, called Officer Kanaapu on the radio. "1J357, dispatch," Sally said in a professional tone that was not normal.

"Dispatch, 1J357, go ahead," the deputy responded, trying to sound like he belonged to a big city cop shop.

"1J100 is calling you on the phone," warning him that the sheriff would call on his cell phone.

Sure enough, in less than a minute, the big boss was on his cell. In the back of his mind, Iawani wondered if he had done something wrong. But as soon as the boss started talking, he knew differently.

"Deputy, we've got a problem down at the Silver Lake trailhead," the sheriff began.

"Yes, sir?" He did not want to interrupt, but wanted his boss to know he was listening. Iawani was headed, lights and siren, back to town and in the wrong direction, so he slowed, thinking he might get to make a turn around with his lights and siren going.

"An older couple from Colorado was coming down the trail when they found the body of a white male in his mid-forties. The couple called dispatch as soon as they got into cell phone range. The EMTs and our detective," (Lincoln County only had one because of the low crime and even lower population,) "huffed up the trail for a couple of miles with the paramedics and the coroner. They found this guy, uh," he paused, clearly looking for his notes. "We found fifty-six-year-old Kevin McFarland of Colorado, clearly dead. Been dead for about two hours."

"So?" Iawani wanted to connect what had happened on the trail with why the sheriff was calling him.

"So, it looked like natural causes. A heart attack or something. With no urgency, we took our time because we didn't want a big shot Colorado attorney trying to claim that a bunch of backwoods peace officers from Wyoming did not know how to do their jobs."

"Yes," said the Island Boy.

"The paramedics and search and rescue volunteers brought the body down in a litter. Sally googled and found his wife's phone number in Colorado. I called. The wife wasn't in Colorado. She was here in Lincoln River, three blocks away in the Lincoln River Lodge, waiting while her husband went on a hike. I gave her the bad news. Then I went over and picked her up to bring her out to the trailhead to identify the body. My wife came along because I was sure this woman would need a shoulder to cry on."

Iawani was more confused than concerned, but he let the sheriff continue.

"We drove her over to the trailhead. As the crew came off the trail and marched into the parking lot, she screamed, 'Where's my son? I thought she was just venting. People come unglued after death notifications, and maybe I just missed her meaning. I told her we would be glad to call him and bring him to her, but she looked at me like I was nuts. She went hysterical, yelling, 'Where's Asher? Is he still up there? Is he still on that mountain?'"

Iawani realized the sheriff was still processing this stunning revelation.

The sheriff's voice changed. "Deputy, we need Nate Garner and that super dog of his, uh—" he stumbled.

"Boo," the deputy filled in the blank.

"Yeah, Boo—to get up there and find this Asher kid before dark. He's a special needs kid. Autism or something. The problem is, Nate is in North Carolina at a search and rescue conference. His dog is here. I know you guys are real good friends and that you know Marie. Can you go over to his house and get that dog and see if you can get the dog to find the boy?"

"Yeah," the deputy said slowly, trying to mask the doubt in his voice. "I could try."

The sheriff did not register Iawani's reluctance. He said, "Bring that kid who helps him train. You know…"

"Caleb"

"Yes, Caleb. Go code. Get here as fast as you can. We need to move!"

So, for the third time in his career, Deputy Iawani Kanaapu drove with his lights and siren blazing down an empty county road toward Lincoln and the home of Nate and Marie Garner. With doors rattling, he pushed the big cop car up to eighty miles an hour, even though every time he hit a cattle guard, it felt like the car was floating on air. With both hands on the wheel, just like they had taught him in the police academy, he told Siri to dial Marie Garner on his cell phone.

CHAPTER 3

Two feet, four paws, and a tail in one pile were all you could see lying in a lump in the grass. It was hard to tell where the boy ended and the dog began. They had played hide-and-seek (Boo's favorite game), and stick (his other favorite game) to the point of exhaustion. After the hard running and the high jumps, the two had piled into the only patch of shady grass they could find to escape the growing heat of the morning sun. Caleb had been the first casualty, dropping to his knees and falling, as if shot, into the cool green blades. He was playing dead. With more energy than a twelve-year-old boy, Boo tried to reignite play, pawing at Caleb's exposed arms. But once he figured out that he could not raise the dead with his paws or cold nose, the bold, handsome golden retriever had succumbed too, laying down with his chin resting in the small of Caleb's back before falling asleep.

You might think Caleb was the luckiest boy alive to have a loyal canine friend like Boo. But it was an earned friendship. Two years previous, Caleb had been dropped off in Lincoln River, Wyoming by his parents, who expected him to live with his Aunt Marge and Cousin Billy. Both treated Caleb like a guest worker rather than a guest, giving him every chore around the house that no one wanted to do. Feeling like a Cinderella, and missing his parents in Iowa, Caleb had run away into the nearby wilderness. For three days, he had been the subject of a massive search that involved hundreds of volunteers. Eventually, Boo had found him, Sheriff Deputy Nate Garner befriended him, and he was returned to the living situation he hated, with one difference. Nate and his wife Marie were Caleb's new best friends, and their hero search dog was his trusted companion. Nate involved Caleb in Boo's daily training routine, and he and the dog had formed a rock-solid bond.

Now, every summer while Caleb's father worked on his doctorate in Iowa, Caleb spent ten weeks in Lincoln River, Wyoming, sometimes sleeping at the home of Aunt Marge but actually living with Nate and Marie, who did not have any children of their own. The "no kids thing" was a topic that was off limits, but once, after Caleb had walked Marie home from church after Nate had left early on a sheriff's call, Marie had tenderly told Caleb, "I hope if God ever blesses us with children that we have a son as precious as you are." He could not tell if she was laughing or crying, maybe a little of both, but as she said those unforgettable words, she tousled his hair, then pulled him to her in an awkward hug.

On this day, Caleb arrived early enough to get Boo out of his crate, where he slept at night. He opened a fresh bag of dry dog food that he found in the pantry and poured out the right portion into the bowl near the back door. Then he filled the other bowl with water. Boo always looked disappointed with his breakfast, but Nate insisted that he be fed only dog food and never people food.

After feeding and playing, Caleb noticed Marie stirring in the kitchen. She'd had a late night, getting home after midnight because she'd had to drive Nate down to Salt Lake City, Utah, to catch his plane. He was attending a search and rescue conference somewhere. Wyoming had two major international airports, Denver and Salt Lake. No matter what, you had to drive a long distance to fly somewhere. He could see the unkept Marie in t-shirt and sweatpants smiling as she worked in the kitchen. There was a phone call, and Caleb could hear her smiling voice from a distance. "Oh, Hi Iawani." Then her countenance changed and her voice became all business. "Yes," she said. "Yes," again. "I'll make them ready."

Marie stepped out on the back porch and called with urgency, "Caleb, bring Boo. There's a search mission." They had played this scene before, with Nate leading the charge. In most searches, people are found pretty quickly, so often, before the truck left the driveway, the search missions were called off. Caleb wondered how this was going to work with Nate in North Carolina. Was Iawani going to handle the dog? Or Marie? She could do it, but Iawani had never been around much during training and Caleb wondered if he knew what to do.

Marie put her hands on her hips. Almost reading his mind, she said in a paced tone, with urgency but no panic, "You are going to have to help on this one, Caleb." She did not ask or command. She just said what was surely going to happen. At that moment, Caleb felt like the third string practice squad quarterback who was called up to start the championship game. But Caleb did not know what the game was, where it was, or who else was on the team.

He looked up to see Boo already bounding his way to the house. Caleb remembered Nate often said, "Boo seems to know when a call-out is coming even before the people do."

Caleb paused and said, "Yes, ma'am."

But Marie had already plunged back into the house and was making sandwiches and filling water bottles, just as she always did when Nate and Boo readied for a search mission. Caleb stepped reluctantly into the mudroom, muffling the spring-loaded screen door against his back as he entered the house. It was just enough sound to tell a busy Marie that he was there.

She began her instructions, "Iawani called." Then she restarted in a slightly more professional tone. "Deputy Kaanapu called. He said there is a missing boy with autism on the Silver Lake Trail. His father died of a heart attack and they think the boy might be scared and hiding nearby. They wanted Nate and Boo, but Nate is gone. So, the sheriff," she paused briefly to let it sink in, "asked Deputy Kanaapu if he could bring you and Boo. He's been around when you train and has confidence in you."

Caleb was not sure if this was an exaggeration designed to boost his confidence, or just the sheriff's desperation, but he knew that there were no other trained search dogs nearby.

Caleb had seen firsthand how little Iawani knew about running a search dog, or about search and rescue. He had occasionally been a willing "victim" when Nate and Caleb had needed a person to get lost for Boo during training. Also, there was another thing that had Caleb worried, though he would say nothing. When Iawani had trained with Nate, Caleb and Boo, he could hardly keep up after 100 yards. The big man could move, but was easily winded in the heat and on steep hills.

Sensing Caleb's worry, Marie paused and looked Caleb right in the eye. "Boo will work for you, and if Iawani stays with you and keeps you safe, then you can give Boo the chance to find this boy. I don't think it will be a hard problem for the dog." Caleb remembered how Marie supported Nate when he was called out in the middle of the night to find the missing. Nate would often say, "Every child is our child," and Marie repeated it.

Marie said, "Remember Caleb, every child is our child, and there is a mother at that trail head who has lost her husband and wants her boy back." Caleb liked, but did not need, the pep talk. He was too busy getting ready.

Caleb reached out and took the sandwich bag Marie had prepared. Back in the mudroom, he took the hiking pack that Nate and Marie gave him for his birthday, the one with the *ten essentials for wilderness travel*, and stuffed the sandwiches in the large compartment. Then he grabbed his jacket and strapped it on the outside of the backpack for easy access, in case there was one of the frequent summer afternoon thunderstorms. He laced on his high-end hiking boots that had been purchased at the local thrift store at the end of the season the year before. Then he turned to ask Marie if she had talked to Aunt Marge to get permission for this assignment that was beyond most twelve-year-old boys. But again, before he could open his mouth, Marie said, "Marge is not answering her phone, and she is one of three people in the world who does not have a cell phone, so the sheriff is going to pay her a visit. Meanwhile, I'm just going to trust that this is OK. I'll call your parents just in case."

Caleb didn't care about Aunt Marge, but he was glad that his cousin Billy would have one more thing to envy him about.

Caleb did not want to blow this opportunity to do a grown-up job in a grown-up way. After all, this was Wyoming, where kids his age were already driving ranch equipment and even pickup trucks. But before he could tell Marie not to worry about his aunt's and parents' permission, he heard the siren of the patrol car in the distance. In what seemed like seconds, the sheriff's cruiser rounded the corner. The sound of the siren brought every neighbor to their window. He was sure that within minutes Marie would receive phone calls from small town residents, overwhelmed with curiosity.

Caleb took the dog's search vest off the coat rack and snapped it on Boo's back. The proud dog stood at attention in the entryway, as if posing for a picture in his uniform that said "Search and Rescue" on both flanks and had a big gold star in the middle. Caleb leaned down and told the canine that this was not a drill. Sensing the emotion, the dog already knew that it was time to work.

As Deputy Iawani Kanaapu came around the corner, he turned off the siren but left the lights on. The big deputy stopped in front of the house, hopped out of the car, and sprinted his bulky frame two steps at a time to the porch of the old, white, two-story house. He was winded as he approached the door. Caleb noted he still had the moves of a football player, but not the endurance.

When Marie stepped onto the porch, there were no pleasantries, just business. She nodded at the approaching deputy while he asked Caleb, "You ready to go?"

Meanwhile, Boo scooted by the 300-pound deputy, leaped off the porch, ran down the pathway, and launched himself into the open back window of the squad car. It was his way of saying, "Hurry, humans."

CHAPTER 4

As the town of Lincoln grew smaller in the rear-view mirror, Deputy Kaanapu turned off the annoyingly loud siren. It was making it hard to speak with Caleb. The blaring noise was also spooking the cows, and the farmers would no doubt complain to the sheriff. But the deputy still drove with haste. Iawani told Caleb all the information he already knew, and Caleb just nodded his head while he thought his own thoughts. His heart and head were spinning from excited, to thrilled, to horrified, and then back to excited. He was one of the "good guys," a valued member of the law enforcement team, on a mission to save a life. This is what his friend and mentor Nate did as a profession, and he wanted to make Nate and Marie proud. He was also thrilled to work with Boo, who was famous enough to get good assignments and some competitive envy. He had complete faith that this superhero dog could track this autistic boy named Asher.

But he was also horrified. They would start the track at the point where the father had died. He might see a dead body. He had never seen a dead body, though he had helped Nate train to find cadavers using old, extracted wisdom teeth. Today, he was going to be tracking a boy described as autistic. He was not even sure what autistic meant. There was an autistic kid in one of the many schools Caleb had attended while his father worked on his graduate degrees and his family moved around the Midwest. That kid had been bullied by some younger kids. When Caleb tried to stop the bullying, the boy just ignored him. A teacher had intervened. "Don't feel bad," the teacher had told Caleb. "That boy has autism. He does not know how to show appreciation." But the next day the autistic boy brought Caleb a homemade cookie in a plastic bag and awkwardly gave it to him on the playground. "You are my friend," the boy had announced, loud enough for all to hear.

That night, Caleb had interrupted his father's study time, told him about the playground incident, the cookie, and his new friend. Then he asked his father about autism. In a rare, open conversation, his father had said, "I have some autistic kids in my class at the junior college. Some of them are really smart. Genius smart. But then they can't spell or tie their shoes. Some don't like to be touched or have a sensitivity to smells, and most do not have good interpersonal skills. But the ones I know are the lucky ones. Some autistic kids are pretty much homebound. They never really leave the care of their parents. So, they can be different. In our teacher training, the one thing I remember they told us is that if you know one autistic kid, you know one autistic kid."

Iawani drove hard and talked loud with the wig wag lights flashing red, white, and blue. The cruiser slowed on the highway and turned east on a dirt road up toward the hills. After a mile, as the landscape changed from sagebrush to trees, they passed a National Forest sign and a marker which said the trailhead was just three miles ahead.

Caleb asked the big Hawaiian deputy what it meant to be autistic.

"I don't really know," he said. "They are special needs, but special needs is just another word for different."

When they arrived at the parking lot, they were instantly greeted by the sheriff who said, "Good, you are here and ready to go." He then handed the deputy a small plastic bag containing a sock, and said, "This is your scent article. Don't touch it unless you have your blue gloves on."

The deputy nodded.

Then the sheriff turned to Caleb and talked to him like he was an adult. "Don't worry about the subject's reaction to the dog. His mom says he is okay with dogs. It's people he doesn't like." Then he turned and walked back toward his vehicle.

I'm a person, Caleb thought, as he lifted his pack off the floor of the cruiser, then looked around for anything he might have missed. Then he tied his boots using double knots. He knew they would go over rough terrain and need to hurry. He did not want to worry about flapping bootlaces.

The deputy handed him a stuff sack that looked like a sleeping bag. "Here, take this," he said.

"What is it?" Caleb asked as he tied the football size nylon bag to the outside of his already full pack.

"It's a bivvy bag," the deputy said. "A lightweight sleeping bag in case we find him, and he needs to be kept warm."

That was when Caleb realized that Deputy Kaanapu did not have a search pack, just a big belt with all the tools of a police officer. A radio, a gun, a Taser, handcuffs, extra bullets for the gun, and a giant key chain. In his chest pocket behind the badge, he had a notebook and a traffic citation book. Heavy stuff that was pretty much useless where they were going. Because of his size and his belt kit of law enforcement essentials, he rattled when he walked. Also, he was always pulling at his waist, trying to keep the weight on his belt from pulling his pants down.

Caleb took the short leash out of his pocket and clipped it to Boo. He left the long fifty foot tracking leash in the car. Boo could track on the long leash and pull Caleb right up the hill, but during training, the long leash always got caught on trees and bushes, jerking the highly motivated dog off his feet. Caleb decided it was best to let Boo track off the long leash as long as possible. He knew Boo would sometimes wait impatiently for the handler at the crest of the hill before going out of sight. And if he made the find, then Boo was trained to come back and get the handler. The return was called the "recall," and was the most essential skill for a search dog.

Caleb planned to keep Boo on the short leash, at least until he had crossed the parking lot that was likely full of doggie distractions, like garbage and well-wishers who wanted to treat Boo like a pet. Boo always looked like he wanted affection, but Caleb remembered the times when his dog magnetized people to come and pet him, and Nate would need to intervene and say, "he's working." Once they were well out of the parking lot and away from well-meaning strangers who might want to pet Boo and interrupt his work, Caleb would give him the "free dog" command and let him off the lead. Then, when they arrived two miles up the trail at the point-last-seen (PLS), he would take out the scent article, initialize Boo, and give him the track command.

Caleb pulled his pack on his back and was ready to go, but he could see that the deputy was hesitating. Sweat was already building up around the deputy's neck as Caleb asked, "Do you think you really need all this stuff?" motioning toward his belt.

"I'm required to carry most of it," he lamented, wondering if the sheriff would notice if he didn't have his full belt kit. Iawani's reputation was at stake, with the sheriff, his colleagues, and the community. He could feel all eyes upon him, and he wanted to do well.

"Bring water," Caleb said, handing him a small bottle of Dasani water that had been rolling around on the floor of the cruiser. "You are surely going to need this." Caleb sounded like an adult scolding a child as he handed the deputy a hat that would protect him from the midmorning sun. "But I'm not sure you will need your Taser and handcuffs. And you *won't* need those extra bullets."

To Caleb's surprise, Iawani took his advice and shed some items on his belt. But even after he shed the items, Caleb could see that his fun Hawaiian friend was not up to chasing a high drive dog up the mountain at 7,000 feet elevation. Of course, to be fair, Caleb thought, most kids from Wyoming would not be up to swimming out to the edge of the reef and riding a wave back to the beach. He could see this island boy was dreading the fast climb up the trail to the PLS and whatever came next. As Caleb and Boo led out across the parking lot and towards the sheriff's SUV, he glanced at the deputy a step behind him holding his trash, with his rattling, now lop-sided belt, and heavy footfalls.

Unlike the struggling deputy, Boo was prancing. He swung back and forth on the leash, waiting for the moment he would hear the relished "search" command. Like most search dogs, Boo could tell right from the start that this situation was for real. He could smell the fear on the humans and hear the concern and urgency in their voices. As they approached the command center in the sheriff's SUV, Boo put his nose half an inch above the hot pavement and created a scent inventory. Caleb had heard Nate explain it this way–

"Humans are visually oriented. Imagine that every time you walked anywhere you left a reflection that stayed bright at first and gradually faded over twenty-four to forty-eight hours. If you arrived in this parking lot, you would see what was there, but also see the faded reflections of cars, people, and animals that had been there and left. It's like visually traveling back in time. That is the world of a dog. Their nose is hundreds of times more powerful than humans, but 70 percent of the brain is also dedicated to their ability to sort smell. They smell objects whose scent lingers long after they have left. So, they work out the smells even before they are given a command to search for a particular scent."

The sheriff knew this too when he planned his search strategy. There were already potentially hundreds of human and animal smells in the area, so adding a large group of SAR volunteers to that number would reduce the chances of the dog finding the right track and making the find. So, he gave the deputy, Caleb, and Boo a one-hour head start.

"You have sixty minutes before I start the team up the mountain," the sheriff said as they approached his SUV. "Those guys," he motioned towards a gathering group of SAR volunteers standing under the pavilion, "are getting restless." Then he looked back at Caleb. "Look," he said, "I have seen this dog work for Nate, and I hope he can work for you. And I want you to know," he made sure he had Caleb's full attention, "that regardless of what happens in the next few hours, the sheriff and citizens of Lincoln County truly appreciate your service, young man."

Caleb loved being called a "young man." His parents, his aunt Marge, his teachers, saw him as a boy. But Nate and Marie, the sheriff, and the deputy saw him as a "young man."

The sheriff smiled, winked and said, "Let's get you moving up the trail before the media gets here and sees that we have a twelve-year-old boy and a dog spearheading this search."

With those words, he was back to being a boy again but, with all the confidence he could muster, Caleb started up the trail, looking past the SAR volunteer group that included trail runners, veteran hikers, man trackers, and tough ranch hands, all ready to launch towards the lake and the mountains. They reminded him of the penned bulls he had seen in the rodeo, waiting to explode out of the gate. But as he passed, he could not help but feel their hot stares as if he was turning, crossing a picket line of a union strike. Caleb could tell that they would do everything they could to catch him, pass him, and find Asher first.

Before they were out of range of the parking lot, the deputy was already twenty steps behind. Caleb glanced to his left and saw an older woman sitting on a log. He paused. She sat still, like she would break if she moved. Her arms were folded, and her dark sunglasses were a vain attempt to hide her emotions. There were tracks of tears on her puffy cheeks, and a used-up tissue wadded in a ball in her hand. She was not dressed for the outdoors except that she was wearing a "Denver Broncos" hat that seemed too large and did not go with her outfit.

With no words being said, Caleb knew who she was. He was not surprised when she called him by name.

"Caleb," she said, "I'm Asher's mom." Her voice was a quiet monotone. Caleb could tell that she was all cried out. "The sheriff said you and this dog can find my boy."

Caleb gave a reluctant nod.

"When you do," her voice turned cautionary, "just be his friend and give him time to figure you out."

Caleb nodded again.

"You have one enormous advantage over those other guys," she motioned towards the SAR volunteers.

"What's that?" Caleb wondered out loud.

"You have this dog," she said.

Boo stretched his leash towards the woman, and she reached out her hand so that Boo could put his cold nose near her palm, then he looked in her eyes for a moment, and licked her fingers. It was his way of comforting without confronting. But it was also his way of checking her scent off the scent inventory list.

Just as the deputy caught up, Caleb said, "We will do our best, Ma'am." Then he turned with Boo and headed up the trail.

CHAPTER 5

Two hundred yards from the parking lot, Deputy Kaanapu was running out of gas. Caleb and Boo were out of sight. His one water bottle was half gone, and a blister was burning on the heel of his left foot, reminding him he had worn the wrong shoes to work that day. The khaki uniform shirt that the deputy paid his neighbor to iron and starch was now wrinkled and drenched with sweat. His pants were dusty, and he was in a battle with his rounded waist that wanted to push his pants down while he wanted them up.

These were minor issues compared to his burning lungs. As the deputy tried to keep pace with the boy and his dog, suddenly the pipes in his throat that were supposed to deliver air to his lungs shrank, accelerating his lungs that were already pumping at capacity. It reminded him of the times as a boy that he would swim in the ocean and reach just a little too far for the lobster or the shell. When he finally popped to the surface, he would suck in air, his lungs pumping and burning. In the ocean wave, where he had been almost every day of his life before he moved to North America, he would recover his air, then swim again even deeper, but on this dry trail there was no recovery. He sucked for air and his pipes dried out, and he wanted water. It was like the worst football practice of his college days, and it was getting worse. He looked at his bottle, already half empty, and realized that water rationing had already begun.

There was a time when Deputy Kanaapu had been in great shape. Football shape. As a big lineman, he would explode off the line to block his opponent or pull and run ten quick steps to open a hole for a runner. But even in his playing days, he rarely ran over fifty yards. After football, he had continued to eat as if he was working out every day, but over time, the calories caught up to him, and mostly stuck around his waist. His weight had kept him from getting job offers at larger police departments, so he ended up in Lincoln County, where recruiting law enforcement officers was always difficult.

Caleb was already going up the switchbacks on the mountain. As planned, he had taken Boo off the leash. The dog was already working, nose to the ground, sorting the list of unique scents. Just like humans can remember a photograph, dogs can remember smells. Some dogs can remember 400-500 different scents.

When Caleb looked back and could not see the deputy, he was worried. Not for the deputy, but because the deputy had the scent article in his pocket. In order to put Boo on the right track when they reached the PLS, Caleb would need the scent article. Caleb wondered how the search would go if he had to wait for the deputy. Boo was used to working fast, and was impatient even with fast humans, when he was on a track.

As Caleb rounded the corner on one switchback, Boo had already found them, scent inventoried them, and moved on. One deputy cheerfully asked Caleb, "Are you Nate Garner, junior?" then laughed.

"Just helping," Caleb said shyly.

"Well, you are about half way to the PLS," he reported.

Then the other deputy inserted, "I thought you were working with Kaanapu?"

Caleb reported he was still down the trail somewhere, and the two stepped by and muttered something about rescuing the island boy before he "gets in over his head" in the Wyoming wilderness.

A few minutes later, Deputy Kaanapu encountered the same two deputies coming down the trail. They were not as friendly with him as they had been with the boy and his dog.

"You look like you are running on empty," the first one said.

Kaanapu held up his now empty water bottle to show that he was out of water, saving his breath for breathing rather than talking.

"Take some of mine." The second deputy opened his backpack and produced three water bottles, then handed two of them to Kaanapu, who nodded a thanks, then continued up the trail. He was too tired for words and too weak to show his embarrassment.

"No pack?" the deputy said under his breath, but Kaanapu did not react. He just faced the trail and the seemingly endless series of switchbacks.

At the top of the switchbacks, Caleb came into the PLS. It was standard procedure to secure the space of an unattended death until it was officially ruled a natural death.

Caleb was relieved to see what he had already heard on the radio. The body of the father had been removed and carried down the mountain by SAR volunteers in a Stokes litter before he had arrived. Caleb found a sliver of shade and called Boo over for a rest and a drink. As he did, one of the fresh deputies said, "I think Kaanapu is going to be awhile."

And he was right. It took another ten minutes for the tired deputy to crest over the hill and into the PLS area. He quickly piled into the narrow sliver of shade where Boo and Caleb were resting. "I'm out of water," he produced the two empty bottles his colleague had given him. "And I'm out of gas," he said honestly. Then in short, breathy sentences he said, "This boy needs to be found. He's probably not too far away. Hiding in the bushes. Here is the scent article. Here is my radio. Keep it on channel 3. That's SAR Ops. SAR operations, I mean. Only call in if you find him. I'll use their radio (motioning to the other deputies) to stay in touch with the sheriff. Good luck."

Caleb was stunned that this heavy responsibility was now all on his shoulders, but he was relieved that Deputy Kaanapu would not be holding them back. Caleb stood and, as he did, Boo came to attention next to him. The dog could sense what was coming and his excitement was growing. Caleb slid open the plastic hinge on the bag containing the scent article with Asher's clothing and placed it in front of Boo's nose. Then in a loud voice he said, "Track!"

Boo wandered around the tree that provided the sparse shade, smelling for a scent which matched the article in the plastic bag. A moment later, he shot up, his nose went down, and he pranced up the trail with a twelve-year-old boy right behind.

CHAPTER 6

Caleb had seen it many times as he helped Nate train Boo to track, but it was still amazing. The scent left hours ago by a young autistic boy was like an invisible rope pulling the dog by his nose up the trail. Sometimes Boo would go from one side to another. Sometimes he would put his nose in a scent trap, like the shade behind a rock, or on a bush, but his direction remained true and his confidence remained strong. If Caleb did not fall behind, Boo did not look back. A few times, Caleb lagged too far behind. When that happened, Boo would stop, wait, and then move on. Because of that, he was rarely out of eyesight.

After about twenty minutes, Boo's tongue hung out. Tracking dogs need a lot of water to keep their olfactory nerve down to the stream and the base of the waterfall. At the junction, Boo seemed a little confused, but then followed the trail to the water. Caleb thought they might get close to the subject, because Boo seemed to slow down. At the stream, the dog waded into the water and sat down. With his nose facing upstream, he lapped at the water, drinking in the cool mountain water while cooling the core of his body.

After a few minutes, Boo rose and wandered over to a large rock. Caleb could see a fresh footprint in the mud by the rock, and Boo put his nose right in the footprint. Then he walked around the rock with his nose down. The dog followed the scent back to the main trail, then continued higher into the mountain.

So much for the quick find at the waterfall. In fact, so much for the theory that the boy was hiding somewhere near the PLS. If Boo was right, and he likely was, the boy was up the trail and probably headed towards the lake.

Caleb wondered if he should report that to Deputy Kaanapu so that he could tell the sheriff, but Boo was hurrying, and he did not have time to take the out the radio and make contact.

As he worked his way up the trail, Caleb noticed something that confirmed they were getting close to Asher. Caleb had heard a detective at the PLS confirm that Asher and his father each hiked with two poles. Investigators believed Asher had likely picked up one of his father's poles, so Asher now had three poles. Two in one hand and one in the other. The tracks in the dirt held two little dots on one side of the footprints and one on the other. They were definitely tracking the right person.

Asher's trail was relatively easy to follow visually up the switchbacks, but soon things leveled out and the steep trail passed over a field of rocks and boulders. Once again, Caleb was relying on Boo to follow scent to source. Without stopping, Boo wove a track through the boulder field, over a short ridge, and into a grassy meadow. Caleb was surprised that they had not yet seen anyone coming down the trail, because this was an especially nice place to be on a hot summer's day when the lake invited a dip.

Caleb remembered when he had gone with Nate and Marie, and of course Boo, to the lake just a few weeks after his own wilderness ordeal, when he had run away and gotten himself lost. It had been his first time back in the woods after three days of survival. He was surprised that his own experience of being lost gave him confidence to be in the natural environment without fear. He hoped that if Asher was feeling lost, he would not be paralyzed with fear.

Boo continued his track, splashing Caleb across the stream and never deviating from the trail. Caleb was glad that Asher was following a trail, but he wondered why he was going toward the lake and not toward town. Why was he moving and not hiding? He knew he was getting closer and would soon have the answer. But before he was out of radio range, he decided it was time to make a call to Deputy Kaanapu and the sheriff.

As he turned on the radio control, he could hear a concerned sheriff say, "You mean you gave him your radio and sent him up the trail by himself?"

Then Deputy Kaanapu, speaking in an apologetic voice on the radio he had borrowed from the detective at the PLS said, "I had to because the dog was really moving, and I couldn't keep up."

There was a pause, and Caleb jumped in. He knew enough about the radio to squeeze the button on the left side with his thumb, pause, then speak. "Caleb calling Deputy Kaanapu." He said it twice, then took his thumb off the transmit button.

"Caleb, come in," the deputy said in a surprised and welcoming voice. Judging from what he had just heard, Caleb assumed that the deputy, while worried about Caleb, was also worried about his career.

Caleb squeezed the side button and spoke again. "We are tracking Asher up the mountain. It looks like he is going to the lake, but I'm not sure." He paused and let go of the talk button.

The sheriff piped in, "Are you sure you are tracking Asher?" There was a pause.

Caleb had heard a lot of police transmissions while riding in the car with Nate. They had their own way of talking, with codes and numbers. Caleb did not understand most of it, but this he understood.

"Pretty sure, Mister Sheriff." Caleb felt stupid for calling him "Mister." Then he continued, "The detective said Asher was carrying three hiking poles and we are following someone using three hiking poles."

"Ten-Four." The sheriff said in a cheerful voice. "Are you code four?"

Caleb had no clue what "Code Four" meant, so he did not respond immediately.

The sheriff self-corrected and said in a softer, fatherly tone, "Are you OK, young man?"

"Yes, I'm fine," Caleb said honestly. "I don't know where this boy is going, but Boo does. And I think we will catch up to him soon."

"OK," said the sheriff. "We have about twenty SAR volunteers who are leaving the trailhead now. Be sure and tell us where you are and when you find him. Talk to us every 20 minutes. Also, keep the radio on so you can hear us calling."

This last suggestion seemed like he was being chastised a little. He wondered how long the sheriff and Deputy Kaanapu had called for him on the radio before he turned it on.

"Ten Four," Caleb said, hoping he could recover some credibility with the sheriff by using police talk, even though he was not absolutely sure he had used the right numbers.

To assure him, the sheriff said, "Ten-Four and out."

Caleb held the radio in one hand so that he could hear the chatter from the others involved in the search, but soon there was more talk than he could track. He turned down the volume and followed the dog across the meadow and into the trees.

In the trees, the actual trail split into many smaller trails, but Boo knew which one to follow. He took the left fork every time. Caleb knew they would end up on the north side of the lake, and that they were not too far away.

As they broke out of the trees, Caleb got his first glance at the lake about a third of a mile ahead, and to his right. On the north side of the lake was a single figure with his back to Caleb, walking around the north side of the lake. Caleb paused and looked carefully. Yes, he was carrying three hiking poles.

Now Caleb could see him, but Boo could not. The dog was so tuned into tracking with his nose that he could not disengage and track with his eyes. He still needed to follow his nose. Now, with the subject in site, Caleb moved with renewed energy. As he huffed through the open country as fast as he could move without running, he took the radio, keyed the mic, and said, "I think we've got him."

Down the trail at the PLS, Deputy Kaanapu pumped his fist and high-fived the detectives. But at the command post, they wanted details before they notified the mother and tossed around a little celebration themselves. The sheriff called Caleb, but all Caleb could hear was a crackling sound and static. He was getting out of range and the batteries on the radio were dying.

CHAPTER 7

The scene looked like a postcard. There was a large green meadow, a blue lake, and a mountain range in the background. The blue sky hung over verdant green grass, and the water reflected tiny starbursts of light as the breeze rippled the water. The only thing needed to make this picture perfect would be a majestic elk posing with a huge rack of antlers. But the elk herds were scattered at this time of year.

Boo came in and out of the picture as he worked the meadow with his nose. He would stop at high points along the way and pose, surveying the land with his big scent-collecting snout, following the scent trail left by Asher. Slowly, indirectly, he was leading Caleb towards the figure standing on the lakeshore.

Caleb assumed Asher had run out of gas and was waiting to be rescued. This has been pretty easy, Caleb thought, as he charted a more direct route across the meadow than Boo had taken. Now all he had to do was get to Asher, explain what was happening, and then figure out how to call the sheriff on the radio. If he could not get the radio to work, Caleb knew the teams of SAR volunteers were coming up the mountain and would easily find him once he blew his whistle three times. They would have radios and could call for a helicopter that would help evacuate Asher off the mountain, or even walk him down to the trailhead.

Caleb's mind wandered into places he knew he shouldn't go. He wondered if he might be labeled a "hero" for finding Asher. That label might push him back into the "outsider" group with kids his own age. Still, he would accept the recognition for Boo's sake and for Nate and Marie, who had worked so hard to train Boo. Perhaps, he would cross the line and become an insider with the SAR volunteers, who had seemed to resent his involvement so far. He imagined they would abandon their skepticism and give him high fives and handshakes for finding Asher.

Then he remembered the parade in town earlier in the summer where he had seen two uncomfortable volunteer firefighters in a convertible car with the mayor, trying to look like they wanted to be there, but wishing there would be a five-alarm fire at the mayor's barn. They were credited with breaking through the locked front door and rescuing a woman and children in her burning home, but some townspeople were critical, including Aunt Marge. They had saved the woman and children, but not the cats. Several had perished in the fire. Of course Aunt Marge, who put cats above all other creatures on the earth, thought the cats should have been saved before the people.

Caleb had once gotten into a "dog versus cat" argument with Aunt Marge. The result was that she had not spoken to him for two weeks. Regarding the training that Caleb helped Nate do with Boo throughout the summer, Marge had said something like, "What's the point? Can't people find lost people?"

Caleb then took it upon himself to inform Marge about all the amazing things that dogs can do that cats cannot. "Dogs can find illegal drugs. They can find bombs. And they can give therapy and comfort. Some dogs can identify when blood sugar is low in a diabetic person. And dogs can identify some cancers, Parkinson's disease, and even COVID. And yes, they are good at finding lost people," Caleb said.

Marge made some statement about cats that Caleb did not really listen to. He was too busy crafting his next line that he landed like a zinger and which caused Marge to storm out of the room and later tell Caleb's mother on the phone that she would like an apology "after all that she had done for him." Caleb's zinger was, "Have you ever heard of a search and rescue cat? Never! Right! Cats would not care if the whole human race was wiped off the face of the earth, as long as they had food, shelter, and a lofty position to look down over their space." As Marge left the room, Caleb, who had not yet developed verbal brakes for his mouth, added, "Besides, Nate says they are just potted plants with paws!"

Perhaps, Caleb making this find of Asher would settle the "dog versus cat" argument once and for all, and he would be declared the winner, and that would bring him into the inner circle of this town where most families had to live for a generation to cross that line. It might be nice to have the SAR volunteers, the sheriff, and even cousin Billy and Aunt Marge congratulate him for his success. He might even get some recognition from his parents, who were a day's drive away in Iowa. It might be nice, he thought for a minute, to hear my father say with approval, "Nice job, son," and my mother say, "We are so proud."

As he was thinking, he noticed Asher was moving again. He had turned and was headed around the lake and away from Caleb. The trail led to the camping area to the right, but Asher was following the lake shore to the left. If he continued that direction, he would be in the dense forest in the back of the lake valley, between the lake and the steep ridge.

Caleb beelined towards the subject, breaking into a trot. Recognizing the excitement, Boo looked over at Caleb, then put his nose in the air. This was like shifting gears for a search dog. When he was tracking, he was working with his nose down, searching for the scent of tiny skin cells left on the ground and the in small disturbances and footprints make in the soil. When tracking, he followed the exact path. But when his nose went up, he was looking for scent blowing in the wind. He could move faster with his nose up, and he did. Outpacing Caleb, he also began a blind beeline to Asher.

As the two sped up across the open green space, Caleb tried again to call the sheriff on the radio, but now the radio was completely dead. He wondered if he had damaged it or turned it off while jostling it in and out of his pack. Perhaps he had accidentally switched channels. He stared at the confusing set of controls on the top, side, and front of the radio. No time to troubleshoot. He had to get to Asher before the boy created another problem by going out of sight and into the dense trees.

Caleb remembered being at the lake a year earlier with Nate. It had been Caleb's first fishing trip and almost his first fish. He had felt a vibration, then a tug on his line. As he'd pulled hard to bring the fish in, the line went slack and all that was left at the end of his line was a hook with no bait. Caleb could feel Asher was getting away, and it was time to reel him in.

It was hard to move fast. The green meadow looked flat and open, but it was rutted with small, rather deep trenches and pools dug by beavers. They were mostly covered by the long grass, difficult to see until you were right upon them. He tried to hasten, but it was more like an obstacle course than an open track. He could jump across the mud holes, but it was hard to tell where the firm ground was on the other side. Several times Caleb misjudged the edge of a trench and found himself with his butt in the grass, or his foot in the mud. After a couple of near face plants, he decided that slowing down would ultimately mean that he could get there faster.

Several times he paused and found Asher's distant figure following the lakeshore, but Asher, as far as he could tell, had not seen Boo yet or noticed that they were closing in. He did not yet know he was about to be rescued. Closer now, almost within shouting range, Caleb could see it was him. He had three hiking poles, one in one hand, and two in the other. He was walking with an unusual gait. Even though he was twenty-six years old, he walked like an awkward teenager who had yet to grow into his body. Caleb could also see that he was fully outfitted with a large, and probably heavy, back pack. He had to be twice as big as Caleb to carry a pack like that. Caleb hoped that this lost person, this man, even though he carried the "autistic" label, would listen to him when he said, "Asher, it's time to stop and wait for search and rescue."

Twenty more labored steps, and Caleb thought he was close enough to be within range of his voice. He cupped his hands and called, "Asher!" There was no reaction from the lumbering autistic hiker with the unusual gait. "Asher, I am here to help!" he cried. "Asher," he said under his breath, now with a tone of frustration.

Asher did not change his pace or direction of travel. He was about 200 yards ahead on the shore of the lake. The dense trees and forest were on his left, and he appeared to be looking into the woods while he walked. It seemed like he was calling to something or someone. Caleb could not hear what he was saying or who he was talking to. It looked like he was having a conversation with the trees.

A few more quick steps and Caleb arrived at the lake shore just behind Boo, relieved to have the tall grass meadow obstacle course behind him. Boo had taken a different strategy getting through the meadow. As a golden retriever originally bred to be a hunting dog, he had woven through the muddy spaces and waded through the pools. This meant traveling a much greater distance, but not having to leap between the islands of grass and risk injury.

While Boo loved the marshy terrain, it also created a rather comic sight. Boo climbed up on a high point along the shore as he closed in on Asher. He posed dramatically, but he was not the noble, stout retriever with a golden blond mane being tossed by the wind that reminded Caleb of the muscle men with their shirts off on the front cover of a romance novel. His legs and stomach were coated in black mud. He was disheveled and motley looking, with splattered mud even on his face.

Caleb did not want him scaring Asher, so he called "wait," then "come," picked up a stick, and heaved the stick as far as he could out in the lake. Normally, Boo would launch into the water before the stick hit. Retrieving was his favorite game. But this time he stood frozen and puzzled on the shore. He looked over at Caleb, then looked at the stick floating in the water.

Caleb realized Boo was still on a search command. Playing was not allowed while the dog was on search command. To relieve the confusion, Caleb said, "Go get it," and Boo shot like a rocket into the water and swam out to the stick.

Once retrieved, he swam in a circle for about ten seconds, then dog-paddled to shore with his nose sticking up like a snorkel, sucking for air. He stepped just out of the water, paused, then did a shake off that sent a spray ten feet in every direction. Caleb was nine feet away, and the shake off sent a fine cooling mist onto his face. Even after a minute or more of shaking, Boo's fur was still wet, making him look thirty pounds lighter, smaller, and certainly not regal. When he was done with his ritual, he picked up the stick and casually dropped it at Caleb's feet, hoping for another toss. When the second toss did not come, he climbed up onto a rock that had collected the sun's heat and rested.

Caleb rested too, just long enough to take a long drink from his water bottle. As he drank, he remembered "reeling in the fish." He glanced at Asher, still 150 yards away, lumbering down the shoreline, talking to the trees. Caleb wondered if he was calling for his father. He wondered if there would be a big emotional scene when he faced Asher and told him to come home.

Then a figure appeared in the shadows of the trees just ten feet from where Asher was standing. The figure was tiny, almost elfin like, but wearing camo pants, a camo jacket, and hood that obscured the face. The person stood looking at Asher, arms extended. Then he reached out, rushing to the surprise stranger and pulling the figure in for a hug.

Caleb called Boo and told him to go "back to work." Caleb could see a Boo's confusion with the command. The dog felt like he had already successfully found Asher, and he had been rewarded with stick play in the water. Now he needed to sort out what was happening down the beach with the stranger. Boo stretched, hopped off the rock, placed his nose in Asher's footprint on the beach, and began a medium gait towards the subject. Caleb shouldered his pack and looked toward Asher just in time to see him disappear into the dense woods.

PART II
OVER THE MOUNTAIN

CHAPTER 8

Marianna! A worried mother wanted to call into the dark forest. But she remained silent and hoping. *Come home!* She wished her heart would guide the young girl home. Already the shadows were gone, leaving the woods a dull gray monotone that preceded the dark. Mother needed to trust her twelve-year-old daughter and wait. No calling. Not even phony bird calls that might alert others.

Then there was movement in the bushes.

Marianna moved with stealth, coming in from a different direction from the last time, so as not to wear an obvious pathway to the hiding place. Her canvas shoulder bag was bulging with berries, and she held two small fish in her left hand. They would eat well tonight.

"The barn hiding place has been discovered," reported the young girl. "I saw the police checking it today."

"Did they see you?" Mother asked, but she already knew the answer.

Marianna looked at her without answering the question.

Mother knew her daughter was practically invisible when she moved through the forest. That's why she sent her daughter, as young as she was, to find food every day. But they were also sad that they had lost the use of this hiding place. It was the only place they hid that offered fresh vegetables that Mother and Marianna had planted subtly around the farm to appear as if they were natural plants. Carrots, cabbage, lettuce, and even turnips, planted randomly along the rock walls and in the open spaces so as not to attract attention.

"They took most of our garden," Marianna reported with a frown.

As a diversion, Mother said, "Let's cook." Then she turned and scurried up a short rockslide, then through the disguised door at the base of the cliff, and into their secret chamber.

Once a mine, then a gypsy hideout, it was now forgotten by the locals. They were confident the police would not find this hiding place, if they were careful to have only small fires and not wear a trail to the door.

Father knew where to come. He had been gone for a week trying to sell the family's few remaining valuables in order to get some money to buy their way out. They had some money that Mother kept in a belt around her waist at all times, even when she slept. But they needed lots of money. Father would not steal, which meant the only way to get the money they needed was to sell the artifacts of their past to build a better future. Father left a week ago to visit the flea markets and shops that the secret police didn't monitor. Marianna hoped he would be home tonight, so they would not need to go on to the other hiding place without him. Not the barn, but the rock house near the waterfall a few miles away. If they moved, they would need to make several trips to carry their precious belongings to the next of their three rotating camps.

In the shelter, Mother took the fish while they both munched on a few berries. She could see the blue stains around Marianna's face framed by her unkept hair, showing that she had filled her stomach as she picked. *Good,* she thought. *She will sleep well tonight.* The fish had already been cleaned, so Mother placed soft, dry wood on the small rock framed fire that was just big enough to not make too much smoke. Then she moved the grill over the heat and lay the fish just above the flames. There were better ways to cook the fish, but this would have to do for tonight.

Neither waited for a fork or a plate to eat the fish. As the skin separated from the flesh, indicating it was cooked, they each pulled off pieces, let them cool, and then ate them directly. They could not afford manners or even sanitation any more. Plates and forks were avoided because they would need washing, and water was needed for other more important things.

When the fish was gone, the two turned to the shoulder bag and devoured the berries. Then they drank water from their flasks and took turns at their toilet outside, always in a different place so as not to leave obvious signs.

"When do you think father will be back?" Marianna asked in a lonesome voice.

It was the same question every night and the same answer. "He will be back when he has what we need."

"What will happen if he is caught?" she asked.

"Your father can talk his way out of anything," Mother said. With that, the two took the old quilt from the bag hung overhead and spread it out over the straw pile in the dirt's corner of the open cave. Then Marianna kneeled with her mother as she prayed silently. When father was around, there was no praying. But when he was not around, Mother called on God to protect him every night. So did Marianna.

Then they rose and washed with the little water they had left, letting the soapy water soak into the mud floor in a corner of the cave. Then they both crawled together under the quilt, placing their backs against each other for warmth.

As the flames died in the fire pit, Marianna's eye drooped, her breathing softened, and she slept.

For Mother, it was not that easy. She had stayed hidden all day, reading from the well-worn books they left in each camp, and watching for intruders from their high perch while she waited for Marianna to return. Tomorrow, they would leave the cave and make their way through the forest to a camouflaged rock. Without her husband, she and her daughter would carry the first load to a hiding place near the rock house. Then they would wait, scout, listen, and watch, to make sure the police or hunters had not discovered that hiding place. If safe, they would return to their current camp and carry another load through woods and over hills to the new space.

Mother had gone to sleep worried for the last twelve years. Just after Marianna was born, her husband, Gregore, had been questioned by the secret police about his political beliefs. After the questioning, their farm had been taken by the state "as a place to train Party members."

For several years the three had lived in the barns and spare rooms of relatives, but the Communists kept coming to the university where father worked and insisting that he vow his loyalty. After all, he was an influential professor at the university, and others listened to what he said. The Communists turned up the heat and eventually made threats against his young family. Meanwhile, telling no one, the young family had moved back to the woods around their remote farm because the Party was not using it for anything except a hunting ground. The Communists were not expert hunters.

After the move back to the woods, Gregore had been let go from the university. He had been told that his math classes were "out of date," and being used by the bourgeois West to corrupt the young Communists. When he was laid off, hundreds of his students had walked out of the university in protest. That didn't stop the math professor from becoming a fugitive. Fortunately, there were more fugitives in Bulgaria than there were secret police to arrest them. Most lived in the city and worked in the underground markets. But Gregore had been raised on a farm, and the mountains were his home.

In the morning, Marianna awoke to the sound of the crackling fire and the sizzling of spicy meats in the frying pan. As her eyes opened, she looked for Mother, but Mother was asleep beside her. Afraid to interrupt what might be a vivid and inviting dream, she stayed still in her bed, eyes barely open, drinking in the aroma cooking on the stove. After a few minutes, there was a sound. Someone was coming into the cave.

Father appeared at the entrance to the cave with an arm full of firewood. Marianna leaped to his arms, and he spilled the wood over the packed mud floor of the hiding place. The ruckus woke Mother, who had welcomed Father in the night when he had arrived with a plan for their future and food for a meal. Delicious food. Fresh bread. Spicy breakfast meats. Eggs. Tea. And even a few squares of chocolate for Marianna. What a wonderful surprise. The feast would begin immediately.

"Did you sell our treasures?" Marianna asked, as she tore into a loaf of bread.

"Yes, I did," father said with sadness in his voice. Marianna misread the sadness, thinking of the family heirlooms, silver candle sticks and a few gold coins that were now in the hands of strangers.

"When do we go?" she asked.

"Tomorrow early, after I rest." He said, smiling. "But we are not going to the cliff house. We will walk for three days. First to Albania, then a boat to Italy and the refugee center. I have found a man who will help us."

"For a price," Mother added.

"Yes, for a price," said Father.

For most of her life, Marianna had lived in other people's houses, in caves, the back of barns and hide-a-ways. For a few years, they had braved the public schools with a false name and phony identification papers. The teachers, and even some students, knew her family was wanted by the Party. Many of them were in the same predicament, or had family members on the run, so teachers and students did not ask questions, and Marianna did not give answers. But eventually Father decided it was too risky for her to be in school, and her parents took over her education. Homeschooling for Marianna was like going from third grade to college, because her father had been a university mathematics professor and her mother had studied English literature before the vice of the police state had tightened and they had fallen from grace. Marianna had to work hard to not disappoint her parents.

Whenever they were not looking for food or patching the shelters, she was learning. During the days, she would sit in the sun, often guided by one of her parents. Father had a stash of books near the old farm, and he would go there regularly, keeping books in all the hiding places. By the time she was twelve, Marianna was fluent in English, had read the works of Shakespeare, and could do college level algebra.

The next morning, the three packed up their simple camp, leaving the books and many of the cooking pots and tools behind. Father said to take only their clothes and the quilts. They bundled what they had on their backs and began walking southwest, through the forests, and along the edge of fields. These were well-traveled routes for smugglers and political refugees, with well-worn trails and campsites along the way. They slept during the day, because they were vulnerable to discovery in the open country that needed to be crossed at night.

Along the way, they finished the bread and other small food supplies that father had brought. Hunger returned to their bellies. Father said they did not have time to find berries and fish. They had to hurry. There were river crossings, and road crossings, and even a rail crossing just before they came to a fence and warning signs where they could go no further. There, Father found a safe hiding place and left Mother and Marianna. Mother was sad, almost weepy. She clung to Marianna like she was afraid. It was not like her.

Father was gone for two hours. He returned with an older man dressed in the robes of an Orthodox Priest. But these robes were old and dirty.

"I am glad to meet you." He focused on Marianna. "But you cannot know my name. You can trust me to keep you safe and help you get to a safe place in Albania. From there, someone will help you get to Italy." He was strange but also sincere. Marianna was surprised that he was talking to her, not Mother or Father.

Then she understood. Father had his head down. Mother was silently crying. Everything was quiet when you were on the run. Noise meant discovery and even death.

Mother handed Marianna her bundle of clothing and bedding. Then she took off her wedding ring and the necklace her grandmother had given her. She put the ring in Marianna's pocket and the necklace around her neck. "There is only money for one ticket, for now," her mother whispered. "Father and I can live here until there is more money. But you need a future." The priest had moved closer to Marianna, and now had his hand firmly on her shoulder. She could see her parents had rehearsed this moment so that erupting emotions would not alert nearby border guards. There were brief, stilted hugs behind contained tears, a kiss on the forehead where her mother's tears ran down her forehead. Then Marianna's parents stepped into the dark woods and were gone.

CHAPTER 9

The priest went first, with Marianna twenty to thirty feet behind. If there was trouble, she was to run back the way they came for one mile, then hold, hide, and wait for the priest to talk his way out and come get her. He would sing a folk song if it was a trap, and a church song if it was OK for her to reveal herself. Most days, they saw no one.

"How could such a well-worn path be so empty?" wondered Marianna. They followed the trail along the disputed border between Albania and Bulgaria, seeing the signs of people traveling the same path everywhere, yet no people. They, too, were hiding from anyone with a uniform. People who looked like they could harm anyone who might report. Anyone.

The trail wound over steep cliffs and across ridges. Only once did they enter a village, and it was so the priest could buy cigarettes. He smoked, then coughed, then smoked again. At night, they slept in old churches, which the priest called sanctuaries. Marianna would wrap herself in the quilt that still smelled like her mother and look up at the sky. She wondered what the sky looked like wherever her parents were sleeping. Then she wondered if she should pray, but the priest never did.

They would eat whatever they could find or carry. Marianna was good at finding berries, bird eggs, and edible plants. The priest sometimes bought bread from the people near the sanctuaries, always arguing over the price. They drank water from streams and wells they found along the way. Only once did Marianna become sick. When she got a fever and started vomiting, they had to stop for a day while the germs from the foul water worked through her system. The priest gave her no sympathy.

Once, they came within a hundred feet of a border patrol made up of young men in green wool uniforms wearing funny looking hats and marching with the same cadence. Marianna and the priest dove off the trail and flattened themselves on the ground, hoping to not be seen. Marianna was sure one soldier at the back of the column had seen her lying in the grass next to a tree. The soldier stopped and tied his shoe and, as he bent over, a chocolate bar fell from his pocket. But he just left it, stood up, and ran to catch up with his mates. When the soldiers had passed, Marianna retrieved the gift and tried to share it with the priest, but he just smiled and said, "This gift is for you."

As they walked from morning light to sunset, she wished she could be two people. One would travel back to be with her parents, who were undoubtedly living in hiding in the Bulgarian woods. Another would travel forward with the man who called himself a priest and find a new life in a safe place. Maybe America, or Canada, or England. Then she would send for her parents, and they would be released from tyranny. They would voyage to a new nation together and live together in freedom.

The priest was a smelly man with many bad habits. He had tobacco-stained fingers, a mop of hair, and never cleaned himself or washed after his toilet. His big robe that dropped below his knees was warm, but also tattered and smelly, especially below the waist where the underbrush had frayed and the mud had caked. He wore a large crucifix made of brass with inlaid jewels around his neck. But he also had a tattoo on his arms that he tried to keep hidden from the girl. His face was crooked, and his big mouth was full of brown teeth and gaps. Many of his teeth had been removed or fallen out.

At first, Marianna had been afraid of him. He looked more like the men she had seen wearing leather and entering taverns than the men she had seen going to church. But over the thousands of steps they took every day, she realized he was absolutely committed to her well-being. He always fed her first. Sometimes he stood between her and danger, and more than once spoke harsh words in a language she did not know to a stranger who looked like they might steal or harm them. Even though he admitted he couldn't swim, he helped her cross the rivers safely, sometimes walking up to his chest in the water.

During their nightly walking routine, they rarely spoke. Silence helped them be vigilant and listen for danger that could come from any direction. Early on, Marianna regularly asked how much farther. The priest would always answer with the same response: "It's not how much farther, but how much longer. It will still take a few days."

So, they did not talk, but Marianna watched. She came to appreciate his ability to know when other people were nearby, even though they could not be seen. As they got closer to the border, several times a day he would say, "Scatter!" in a hushed voice, and the two of them would find separate hiding places and watch groups of others pass.

Curious, she asked him how he knew when other people were nearby. "The birds tell me," he said. That sounded like rubbish, but then she watched him. He would stop and listen, and when he heard a change in the background noise in the forest, he would send them both into hiding. Over time, she too came to know when others were near, by listening to the changes in bird noises and hearing the squirrels chirp a warning.

After more than a week and several hundred miles, they came into more open spaces. Farms and fields, with rock walls between the crops. One day, on a sunny late morning, she heard the noises change. Time to stop? To scatter? She wondered why the priest did not react. He kept leading them forward, down the hill. Then there was the sound of an engine, and a swish, and Marianna realized they were approaching a well-traveled highway. It had been so long since she had heard or seen a car or a truck.

The priest was not anxious about being discovered on the open road and, before long, a driver with grease-stained coveralls came by in a truck and stopped for them. Once again, the priest spoke in a strange language. After negotiations, hand gestures, and the payment of money, the priest motioned for Marianna to get into the truck with him. Down the road they went, as the trees and the trail fell into the rearview mirror.

After a few minutes, the driver produced a green glass wine bottle that was half full. He pulled the cork off with his teeth and offered it to the priest, who took a hardy drink and passed it back to the driver. This continued for miles as the two passed the bottle back and forth while Marianna watched. As the wine bottle moved between them, they talked like brothers. Once the elixir was gone, the priest dozed. Marianna, ever vigilant, worried that the driver might, too. After many miles that saved Marianna and the priest hundreds of miles of walking, the driver turned up a steep road. With gears grinding and engine straining, he crossed a road in an open wheat field and found his way to a large church with a rock gate. He stopped at the gate and motioned the two passengers out. Thanks were given to the driver, and he turned around and headed through the field and down the mountain. Then the priest rang a large bell which hung from the gate.

It took several minutes before a pair of women dressed in black and white robes wound their way from the church down to the gate to meet the priest. As they did, the priest took off his cross and removed his robe, revealing an ordinary looking peasant man in a dirty shirt and worn out pants. It made sense that he was not actually a priest. In the time they had been together, she had never seen him pray, recite a scripture, or do anything that was priestly. As the nuns approached, she looked at him and boldly said, "You are not a priest, are you?"

He smiled a weak smile but did not verify her conclusion either way. It was their last conversation, though she would think about his rough and kind manner for the rest of her life.

The nuns approached the gate and told the man in that strange language to step back. He talked with them and motioned towards Marianna, then he took a large sum of money from a money belt that hung loosely around his waist and handed them the entire contents. They took it, but then one sister carefully counted out a few bills and handed them to him.

He willingly accepted, then turned to Marianna. "These are Roman Catholic sisters. This is their abbey. They have ways to get you across the sea to Italy. When the door opens, they say Italy will let you in. Meanwhile, they will take care of you."

Marianna was surprised as the sharp emotions of abandonment flooded in. "You're leaving me?" she asked.

The man stood back as the two sisters stepped out of the gate and surrounded the girl. He smiled, then took two quick steps forward and kissed Marianna on the forehead.

The nuns turned the girl and guided her through the gate. As the gate shut behind her, she heard the background bird noises change as he walked towards the main road with his priest robe bundled under his arm.

CHAPTER 10

So began the time at the abbey. For the first time in her life, Marianna was fed every day and every meal, except Sundays, when there was a morning fast. There were other young girls in the abbey school – some from the village who went home every night, and some who were being boarded in the drafty dormitory that seemed like a luxury hotel to a young girl who had grown up living in the woods. Most of the nuns in the abbey did not talk. They had taken a vow of poverty, chastity, and silence. Some were very kind to the young girls and smiled when they passed. Others had a sharp tone in their gaze.

But the novice nuns — the young ones — were the teachers, and they could talk. A few of them spoke English, but none of them spoke Marianna's native language of Bulgarian.

They also varied in mood. Some were constantly looking to catch young girls breaking or bending the rules. Then there would be threats and even punishment. Punishment began with missing a meal, but repeat offenses would lead to corporal punishment and eventually isolation. Some teachers protected the girls from stone-faced nuns who seemed set on finding rules-breakers. Marianna saw the secret police mentality within the abbey. There were the targets, the defenders, and the punishers, with the vast majority of girls turning a blind eye to it all.

Eventually, Marianna settled into a happy routine. After morning prayers, which the teachers attended but Marianna did not, she dove into books and learning. None of the teachers had better math skills than she did, so she became the unofficial math teacher, further cementing her quantitative prowess. While her colleagues went to English class, she had a private lesson to learn Gheg, the official language of Northern Albania. Often these language sessions turned into interesting conversations with the junior teachers who had entered the abbey under pressure from parents to get away from an unwanted situation involving a boy. While they dressed in black and white, lived in a small communal building, and ate meals with their students, most rarely mingled with the older sisters who seemed to aimlessly float around the abbey like silent ghosts, smiling or frowning at the girls.

When the Gheg language lessons were over, there was a lunch of soup and one slice of bread. Most students complained about the quality and quantity, but Marianna welcomed any nutrition that arrived regularly without effort on her part. Morning meal was usually sweet milk and thick crusted bread left over from the day before. Or mush. The evening meal was in-season: garden vegetables, potatoes, and a scant portion of meat or chicken—except on Fridays, when they had fish. It was this way every day except Sunday, when they skipped the morning and noon meal, and would sit and eat with all the sisters in silence in the big room next to the chapel. This meal was prepared by the women in the local village, and it was always the best meal of the week, with fresh bread and second helpings. Since it was only one meal, Marianna learned to keep a few pieces of bread wrapped in her quilt so that she did not go hungry.

It did not take long for Marianne to feel safe in this sanctuary, but she also learned quickly that the sisters of the abbey lived like they were under siege. They had almost no contact with the outside world.

On her weekly walks in the woods, which she could only do on Saturday afternoons, she was warned never to talk to a Muslim man. Men with beards were evil, and would likely take you places and do unthinkable things to you if you did not run away. Orthodox Christians, like the priest who had brought her to the abbey, were the other group. They were misguided, but not dangerous. As Christians, they were second class. Speaking with them was allowed if it involved normal, practical, everyday things. But the girls were not to speak of the Pope (whoever that was), the Vatican (wherever that was), or tell them anything about what went on in the abbey. It was all about maintaining the mystery, concluded Marianna.

Even without her connections to the Church, Marianna thrived in the abbey. She had friends for the first time in her life: people she cared about, and who cared about her. People she could talk to, even though the heartache of being abandoned by her parents was always just below the surface. She wondered if she could find the path home to Bulgaria. In her fantasy mind, it was just a day's walk away, back to the cave or the cliff house where her parents were hiding. But in her rational mind it was a long and confusing two week walk through dangerous spaces. She did not think she could do it without the man who called himself a priest, which she realized was a false identity for her protection.

Time passed, as it does for happy children, one step away from adulthood, and Marianna grew both socially and physically. A year and six months into her stay, there was a strange request. One of Marianna's favorite teachers named Sister Amaris, who Marianna trusted, asked her to bring her quilt on the field trip. "We will need it to have a picnic on," she said in a phony voice. "and put a spare set of clothing in it because we might get wet," she added. A small class of select girls was going on a field trip to the fish docks in a village nearly a half day away by bus. Sandwiches of goat cheese and cucumbers had been prepared for all the teachers and girls, but Sister Amaris and Marianna were each given two. Marianna was so excited to see the sea for the first time in her life that she thought nothing of the strange request to bring the quilt and the clothes.

The bus for the field trip took them up a windy mountain road, then stopped at the top. The blue Mediterranean was before them. It was as beautiful as she had imagined. Blue, then green, then silver and blue again. It like the leaves on the trees as she looked down on the waves. Scattered around the village small port below them was a collection of small vessels that bobbed on the moving tide.

In the village, they were joined by the students from another school. They saw the fish market. The odor reminded her of the small fish she would catch while living in the woods with her parents. They were ushered into a building by the Catholic Church and given a lecture about the benefits of fish and why the Pope wanted them to eat fish on Friday. Later in the day, a man in a uniform, the kind Marianna had avoided all her life, questioned the school leaders and cautioned them not to board the boats. All the time, Marianna was told to hang onto her quilt and her clothes, and stay close to Sister Amaris.

As they walked down the dock, trailing behind the schoolgirls, a sailor stepped off a boat behind them and said something in Italian. Without words, Sister Amaris motioned to Marianna to follow. The sailor pulled them onto the boat and immediately they were taken below deck, to the front of the boat, through a secret room where the fish were stored. Once below deck, Marianna was told repeatedly to not make any noise, no matter what happened. The door was shut, and the darkness was complete. Sister Amaris took Marianna's quilt, the one that had been her warmth in the winter wood, the one she had carried across the mountains and ridges, the one she held every night and hoped to find the smell of her father and mother, and she pulled it over both of them and said, "It's going to be all right. In two days, I'll be in the Vatican and you will be in a refugee camp, getting ready to go to America."

CHAPTER 11

The fish smell had never really washed out of the quilt. Neither had the smell of Mother's perfume, or the water stain from crossing the river with the priest. That is why it was still so important to Marianna a quarter of a century later. The quilt contained her memories. And now, after failing to make it in America, she was back to living in the woods, finding security in the isolation most people feared. Her quilt was the constant in a variable world.

She had survived the crossing to Italy in a forward fish storage compartment with Sister Amaris, wrapped together in the quilt and shivering with the novice nun who cried and prayed out loud as the waves of the Adriatic Sea battered the hull. When they finally arrived in Italy, bonded by their suffering, there was another abandonment. Sister Amaris went to the Vatican, and Marianna was taken to a refugee camp. Because she was young, small, and vulnerable, the refugee authorities were careful. There were nefarious groups looking for girls to feed their human trafficking network. Marianna could not even go out on the street alone. Isolated again, she was kept with other young girls in a dormitory tent with a wire fence around it. They were well fed, at least by Marianna's standards, schooled, and once or twice a week taken to a beach where they could swim.

During this time, Marianna focused on learning Italian. She kept a journal and made friends with other young and vulnerable girls who were wandering the world without a home. Of course, she wanted to write to her parents and tell them she was safe and working hard, but she feared that sending a letter to any address or any relative would alert the secret police that they were still alive. She did not know that her father had already been captured and killed, and her mother was living with relatives under a different and new name.

Of course, everyone in the camp had hoped to find a place somewhere, with someone. Most did not have a full picture of where their own families were or why they were being kept behind a fence in a tent, isolated from what appeared to be a friendly population. Despite the isolation, Marianna was learning Italian and was the only person who spoke English in the group of girls. She also spoke Bulgarian and Gheg. Her language skills brought her privilege and access as she became the unofficial translator for the UN workers.

It was during this time that Marianna met an American woman from the United Nations Refugee Agency. The woman was especially drawn to this young woman who was a survivor and one who was willing to learn and serve. As a result, Marianna was recommended for adoption and immigration into the United States: the country all the refugees wanted to go to. It did not take long for potential parents to write letters. It felt very awkward because Marianna believed her parents were still alive. But if pretending to be an orphan helped her get to America, then she could play that role.

And play the role she did. When potential adoptive parents came, she marshaled every bit of charm she could to impress them to bring her into their family. The first potential parents were not fooled. "There is something off," one potential mother told Marianna's American advocate. "There is something she is not telling us," or "She has anger management issues."

She was not telling about her scared heart. Every person she had ever known — her grandmother, her grandfather, her village friends, her mother and father—all had abandoned her. Then, in the abbey, after the boat ride, even in the refugee camp, the history of abandonment led to raging nightmares and emotional indifference.

After a year, most of the young girls and all the aid workers in the tent refugee camp had moved on. There were unfamiliar faces all around. She had the reputation as the older, wiser, jaded girl, who was unwanted by potential foster homes and/or parents looking to adopt. But eventually the rescuing angels came for Marianna. An aid worker said there were some American parents who were coming for her. They had read her file, seen her picture, and wanted her. It took several weeks for the papers to process, but one day the phone rang, the aid worker came, and Marianna placed her few, meager belongings in the backpack that she had been carrying since she first started her journey at age 12, and followed her new "parents" out of the fenced enclosure and into a new life. They had tried to get her to leave her quilt behind, but Marianna would have rather left her right arm. She clung to the worn, torn, and dirty cover. The first stop was the US Consulate and then the airport. Along the way, she had to pretend to care and connect, saying "thank-you" and "please" as often as she could, seamlessly transitioning between English and Italian.

At the Giovan Battista Pastine International Airport in Rome, the security people tried to get her to place her quilt on the x-ray machine. Not understanding any of the procedures, abandonment panic took over. There was screaming and shocked looks on the faces of all the adults. Quickly, a female security guard from the airport police intervened. Marianna saw in her eyes a friend.

The friend spoke to her in Bulgarian and said, "I can see you are from the country of my birth. You are going to a new home. You are afraid. I was once where you are now. Please, just let us take a picture of your cherished quilt in the x-ray machine and then I will return it to you."

Slowly, trust took over, and Marianna loosened her grip. The quilt went through the x-ray machine, and the new parents were now hoping to get it through a washing machine.

The plane launched into the sky, and Marianna was thrilled. She had seen such vessels leave trails in the clouds. Now she was on one. But before long, there was a woman in a uniform asking questions, and her fears took over again. "What can I get you to drink?" the woman asked. Apparently, in this new world where Marianna was going to live, the police doled out drinks and peanuts.

Then she discovered that there were movies like the ones they would see on Saturday night in the refugee camp. But before she could figure out the process for watching a movie, her eyes got heavy, her chin slumped, and she was asleep.

The rest of the journey was a blur. They landed in New York. More police and people in uniform. Then they boarded a flight for Grand Rapids, Michigan. In the Grand Rapids airport, her new parents had planned to have a large welcoming greeting, with the extended family and some members of their church. But the counselor in the refugee camp had warned against that. They suggested Marianna would already be overwhelmed by everything. And she was, even though she pretended to care and connect.

The friction in her new family began almost immediately. Her new sister, who was the same age and would be in the same grade, was less than welcoming. The church community that Marianna was expected to attend on Sundays was both naïve and threatening. Naïve, because so many pretended to know where Marianna had come from, yet they had never been hungry, wet, and without. They told stories about "having a friend in Jesus," but they had never been chased by the police or abandoned by family and friends.

The school that Marianna went to, where her sister was already connected into a social group, had nothing to offer. She did not know how to make friends. She had no interest in sports, cheerleading, or the performing arts, and the classes were boring. After a failed semester, the school forced her into a series of tests, and her new parents suggested, before they had seen the results, that Marianna be held back a year or maybe even two so that she could catch up with the others. But the school counselor had a different idea. "We need to get this girl into college as soon as possible before she dies of boredom."

Because her new parents had only saved for their biological children's college, the only option for Marianna was a local community college. It took her a year to complete two-years' worth of work with honors and a string of professorial recommendations that would make any parent blush with pride. But by then, the rift between her and her new family had already grown to the point of no return. The family members, and the parents, expected more appreciation from this refugee girl they had rescued. Marianna did not offer appreciation to these people who wanted to be called her parents, her brothers, and her sisters, but who did not know her or understand where she had come from and who she was becoming.

Her American family only learned that she was graduating from junior college when they offered to help with tuition and Marianna said she was graduating.

"What's next?" her new father asked, somewhat sarcastically.

"MIT," she said, straight-faced.

He did not believe her until she began asking how to get to Massachusetts from Michigan. Then he asked, "How are you going to pay for that?"

"Scholarship," she said. "Full ride."

Helpless to help her, and over considerable objections from her other siblings who were approaching driving age, her adoptive parents took the title of the "kid's car," the old clunker used for the family's teenage drivers, and signed it over to Marianna. "That way, you can come home to see us at Christmas or in the summers," they said. But they knew she never would, and she never did. To avoid being abandoned by them, she was doing the abandoning.

A school like the Massachusetts Institute of Technology privileges reclusive students with obsessive work habits who are happy to eat the food from their meal plan and do homework on weekends. Marianna was so obsessed with school and learning that she dreaded holidays and even weekends when the computer labs were not open, and she could not call her professors at home with questions they had not likely thought about.

Her scholarship did not pay for summer school, so she took a job at a start-up company, only to find out that she knew more than anyone about the programming problem that was at the heart of the business model the entrepreneurs were trying to promote. However, her technical skill did not make her a hero. Fearing for their jobs, others on the development side of the business began undermining her work and claiming credit for what she did. This was a pattern that would repeat throughout Marianna's meteoric career. When the summer ended, she was glad to return to the classes. She used the money she had made to pay for summer school the next summer and graduated a full year early with five job offers.

Of course she did not go to graduation. That was for people who had not been abandoned by their families. When asked about her adoptive family, she gave a lame and only partially true excuse. "I have not seen them in three years. I'm sure they don't care. I think they have moved on." But they did care enough to send birthday and Christmas cards, which she ignored.

After graduation, Marianna started a career pattern of success with technical problems and failure with people. She would accept a job at a tech company where she would be assigned difficult programming problems. She would immerse herself in the work but ignore the people and the politics. Her colleagues would reach out and she would rebuff them. She did not trust anyone, especially her bosses, so she would go over their heads. Eventually, she would find herself face-to-face with a boss or someone in the Human Resources department who would try to fix her. Instead of trying to improve her interpersonal skills, she would work harder and solve more technical problems, hoping to be recognized. But she was not. Her shining brilliance as a computer developer and programing architect went unappreciated by those who wanted her to get along. She would leave or be fired, find a new job, and start over.

In this way, she worked with five different firms over twelve years, finally ending up in Denver, Colorado, working with a company that had a contract with NASA to program the next version of the Mars Rover. There she worked for seven years straight because in this job Marianna could work in isolation, with her boss giving her technical problems to fix, collecting her work, and protecting her from the social buffetings. His name was Albert, and she came to think of him as an uncle, brother, friend, and coworker. Not only did he understand her work and value her contribution, he kept her out of meetings and away from organization currents that would drown her.

The scars of abandonment began to heal, and with that, she developed a life outside work. Though she had no real friends, she would go hiking in the mountains around Denver on some weekends. Then the news came that Albert had retired. Marianna did not have a concept of retirement because she had come from a country where you worked until you died. They had a retirement party, and she went to the party, but the same thing happened at the party that happened when the customs officer tried to take away her quilt in the Rome airport. There was a panic as the wound of abandonment was reopened. The scene she made at the party, the verbal abuse she leveled at almost everyone in the room, was written off as drunkenness, even though she did not drink alcohol. But it was a sign of what was to come.

Marianna's new boss was put on alert. He did not understand her like Albert had, nor did he protect her. After another argument one day, she went home to her apartment, packed all of her possessions—which fit in the trunk of her car—placed the keys of the apartment on the kitchen table for the landlord, and drove north to Wyoming. When she saw the mountains near Lincoln River, she turned off the highway, passed the National Forest sign, and ran out of gas.

Leaving her car at the side of the road, she shouldered her pack, the same one she'd had as a child, loaded a medium size duffle bag, took her quilt, and walked the remaining three miles to the trailhead and into the mountains. This would be her new home, her new family, her new safety. They would not abandon her, but keep her safe from the people in the world who wished her harm.

CHAPTER 12

The sheriff thought the search had been going well and would be over soon until Deputy Kanaapu called in on the radio to admit that he was no longer with the boy and the search dog.

"I could not keep up with them, boss," the rookie deputy said.

The sheriff hated being called boss. He was in command, but he was not the boss.

Between giant sucks for air, the deputy communicated on a radio borrowed from officers at the scene where the body had been found, that he had lent his radio to Caleb—who was hot on the boy's trail. He also said that the missing boy was not hiding near the PLS, as expected, but had headed further up the mountain towards the lake. So, after speaking with Deputy Kanaapu, the sheriff gave the order, and the SAR volunteers headed up the trail. He trusted this team. They had searched this area before and would make a quick exit.

After about an hour, on the sheriff's department SAR frequency, he heard a youthful voice say what sounded like, "I got him." It was garbled, but the excitement came through.

Had he found the autistic boy? Were they both OK? He tried to communicate, but the radio coverage around those mountain peaks was unreliable. He checked in with the SAR team and they had just passed the waterfall and were about an hour from the lake. Not far behind. The sheriff imagined, after paperwork, he would be home in time for supper.

But then a brand-new four-wheel-drive pickup truck with all the whistles and bells drove into the parking lot. It had an array of antennas flopping in the wind and was followed by an older van. Both were light green and had the logo of the National Forest Service on the side.

A short man in a spotless uniform stepped out of the lead truck and beelined for the command center. His enormous round hat seemed to make enough shade for three people.

"It takes a special person to be proud to wear a hat like that," the sheriff chided Chief Ranger Rondo McFee.

McFee was the regional head of several massive patches of National Forest in that part of the state. Whenever he showed up to a big event like this one, where multiple agencies were involved, he wore a round "Smoky-the-Bear" hat and an army green jacket cut at the waist that made him look like he had just stepped out of the 1930s. But the hat revealed plenty about McFee. It was clean, even new looking. So was the chief ranger's uniform. None of the other people in the mobile command center had clean hats. Even the sheriff spent more time in the field than McFee, who just showed up for potential media events and parades.

Of course, local law enforcement, even the volunteers, were suspicious of the federal employees who made more money, spent less time at work, and had better equipment than they did. Technically, the Forest Service had jurisdiction over a search at Silver Lake, but even with the regional ranger calling all hands on deck, only five rangers were available, and only three were qualified law enforcement rangers.

Suspicious that the chief ranger had brought a small team into this search, especially when they were not really needed, the sheriff asked, "What brings you up this way, Rondo?"

But the chief ranger ignored the question and started looking at the maps in the mobile command center. He was sure he had a complete picture of what was going on with the search because he routinely monitored the search and rescue frequency on the radio.

"The coroner seems to be taking their time," Chief Ranger McFee complained.

"It's the detective," the sheriff clarified. "He's taking his time and trying to get everything right."

"So, this might not be an accidental death?" McFee asked, worried that if it was declared a crime, his team might need to work overtime.

"Hardly," the sheriff said. "The man had a history of heart problems, and he was pretty overweight. The only thing that is slowing down the release of the body is that there were two sets of footprints found next to him."

"Two?" the ranger queried.

"Yes," the sheriff responded. "His son's prints were all over the place. But it looks like a tiny person—probably a woman—was also there. We're guessing she showed up after Asher left. We're trying to sort it out." The sheriff wondered why this federal officer who spent most of his time behind a desk was interested in an important but routine search-and-rescue operation.

"Damn. It's her again." McFee turned to the sheriff, his face equal parts exasperated and annoyed. "We think there is a woman living in the woods near Silver Lake. We have had reports for over a year from people who claim to have seen an elf-like creature in the trees and the rocks."

"Elf?" the sheriff asked. Then, still waiting for disagreement from McFee, he repeated, "Elf?"

"Well, she is tiny and dresses in camo green," McFee disclosed. "We've got some drone video of her."

"Drone?" The sheriff was surprised.

"Yes. Because we only have one law enforcement officer for every hundred thousand square miles of National Forest, we are using drones to check out complaints."

"So, you had complaints about an elf?" the sheriff said with a smile.

Dodging the ridicule, the Chief Ranger repeated in an important tone, "We think there is a woman of small stature who is living somewhere near Silver Lake. Some campers have seen her cleaning up camp sites and looking for food. Others have seen her fishing in the streams. One of our rangers, who specializes in investigating ATV accidents, said parts from wrecked vehicles have gone missing, like somebody is scavenging, or even just cleaning up."

"Sounds like a crime to me," the sheriff said with sarcasm. "Has she hurt anyone? Damaged any property?"

"That's the strange thing," the Chief in the round hat admitted. "She seems to take care of the place. We want to know who she is and why she is doing what she is doing. We don't want a group of squatters on federal land."

"I think it's an elf with a driver's license," the sheriff said. "About a year ago, we impounded a car along the road registered to a woman in Colorado. We thought little about it at the time because no one had reported her missing, and the tow truck driver said the car was worth less than a thousand dollars. But then our detective, who does not have a lot of work to do, called the previous owner of the car in Michigan. It was an elderly couple who said they had given it to their adopted daughter twenty-one years ago. They said she's not dangerous, but suffers from anxiety, depression and paranoia. They said she might be homeless. And it sounds like she had a rather interesting past. She grew up in the mountains of Bulgaria. But we couldn't do anything about the car. There was no evidence that she had gone into the woods, and there are no laws on our books about going on a one-year camping trip."

"There are on the National Forest books. Our regulations prohibit stays for over fourteen days. I think she had passed her stay," the chief said with authority in his voice.

The sheriff countered, "Well, she might have moved camp sites every fourteen days. You would be hard pressed to get a judge to charge her with a federal crime. So, let's go easy on her."

When the chief ranger did not respond, the sheriff added, "Let's just try to get her the help she needs if we run into her on this search."

"Off course," the Chief Ranger said dismissively. "I hope you don't mind if I send my team up the mountain as well, just in case there is an encounter."

Feeling the direction of the political winds, the sheriff agreed. But he had been in law enforcement long enough to know when he was not getting the full story from the self-important man in the spotless uniform.

CHAPTER 13

We might lose him again, Caleb thought. That would be humiliating.

Once Asher had stepped into the woods, Caleb and Boo had dashed down the lake shore, overshooting the opening in the thick brush. But Boo's nose and Asher's footprints brought them back to the right place. Asher was well ahead of them now, and probably moving quickly. The dog was working the problem, and disappeared into an opening in the dense undergrowth that was covered with a thick, high canopy of trees. Caleb followed, but then found it was hard to move forward because his eyes had not adjusted to the deep shadows created by the layered foliage. He could not see which direction to go.

Stepping into the dense forest was like going from day to night, and hot to cool. Along the lakeshore, in the dry sand, Caleb had felt the sun-cooked grains through his boots. Once he stepped into the woods, the path was cool, but the soggy ground was slippery.

Twenty feet into the forest, Caleb sat down on mossy deadfall surrounded by ferns and other underbrush to let his eyes adjust. Gradually, his new environment became visible. The ground was covered with creepy crawly things that never saw direct sunlight and probably never dried out. Moss grew on the sides of trees and on the abundant deadfall that blocked any rational path through the forest. Caleb could see he would go around some obstacles, and over or under others.

The meadow leading up to the lake had been an obstacle course with water traps. This one featured deadfall everywhere, and water traps of brown tannic water. But there was a pathway worn mostly by wildlife that made their way to the lake for a long drink every night. When his eyes had adjusted, Caleb could see deer footprints and scat as he followed the narrow path. Nate had taught Caleb to man track to affirm what Boo was tracking. Caleb was pretty good at it. Then he saw a fresh human footprint. It was not Asher's. He had been tracking Asher for two hours and knew his footwear by size and print. This was a small, tiny print, with worn tread. It was a woman's gait, but the prints belonged to someone who was less than 100 pounds.

In a few steps, Caleb saw another foot print. This one was Asher's. He was headed in the direction that Boo was leading them, deeper into the forest.

This is so weird, Caleb thought. *The kid is running away, or running to something, or someone.* Then he remembered the time he had run away and said to himself, "I know something about that," realizing the person he was sent to rescue might not be in his right mind.

It took Caleb thirty minutes to go less than 200 yards. Fallen trees blocked the way. Several times he caught his pack on branches, and was jerked backwards like he had been grabbed by the tree. He went over and under, and sometimes around, all the time getting dirtier and muddier.

He lost the trail several times, but Boo would appear just in sight, urging him on. Caleb would go to where the dog was standing and find a footprint or a broken branch or other sign they were still on the right track. The dog was amazing. Several times Caleb heard movement to the front or side. The chaotic movement generated fear, but Caleb shoved the emotion down. It had to be a wild animal fleeing his own invasion of this secluded place where people did not come.

After a short distance that was crossed with considerable effort, the ground started going up. There was less moss and less moisture as the underbrush thinned.

In front of him, maybe sixty to seventy feet, he could see an opening big enough for sunlight. As he approached, he could see Asher moving back and forth between shadow and light.

What was he doing?

Closer. Soft footsteps.

He could see Asher had already set up the tent. The door of the tent was open, and there was a pad and a sleeping bag carefully laid out inside. Water bottles were carefully arranged on a log near the fire which Asher was getting ready to light.

This was clearly a campsite that was used often for those who knew where it was and wanted to be isolated.

Boo ruined the planned approach by bounding into the opening, running right up to Asher and dangling his tongue, then returning to Caleb for the required recall. Caleb praised quietly, then said, "Show me." Boo then bounded back to Asher, who acted as if the dog was invisible. He would do that three times before Caleb could make himself seen to Asher. As he entered the opening, he expected to see surprise on Asher's face, but the boy was focused on his task. He was making a fuzz stick to start the fire and ignoring his rescuer.

"Asher," Caleb said in a soft voice.

Asher did not look at him or acknowledge him.

"Asher," he repeated. "I am your friend."

Both he and Boo were ignored, making the dog suspicious, even nervous.

"Boo is your friend." Caleb kneeled down and praised Boo, looking up to see nothing from Asher. "We are here to help you."

Still, Asher focused on his task.

"I am sorry about your dad." Caleb wondered if he had gone too far, but there was still no reaction. "I met your mother down at the trailhead. She wants you to come home."

Caleb paused, and before he could try another tactic to get Asher to acknowledge him, there was an unexpected voice from the shadows. A woman's voice. "He cannot understand you. He does not have room in his brain right now. There is too much going on," The voice had a slight accent that Caleb could not place. "Give him time. He will warm to you."

Caleb stepped back in surprise. He turned and looked toward where the voice was coming from. Standing just beyond the light, merged into the shape of a tree, almost invisible and certainly inconspicuous, was a small woman clad in camo, with short cropped hair and a crooked hat. This was the creature who he had glimpsed on the lake shore and whose footprints he had seen in the forest. Caleb realized that he had walked right by her when he entered the clearing and had not seen her. She did not move when she spoke, and her green-on-green wardrobe made her look like an elf.

"Who are you?" Caleb asked.

"I'm Marianna," the woman said.

CHAPTER 14

Caleb studied Marianna, and she studied him, though she had been watching him from afar for some time now.

"How do you know Asher?" Caleb asked.

There was a pause. Her head moved, and she looked at Asher with affection. "He is my friend," she said, loud enough for Asher to hear. Without making eye contact, Asher smiled a weak smile.

"How did you meet?" Caleb continued the inquiry with genuine curiosity.

"He came to the lake many times with his father," she whispered, in an accent Caleb could not identify.

"His father is dead." Caleb said.

"I know," she said. "I arrived too late to help. That is because I was watching from the waterfall." Caleb wanted more detail about that answer, but he moved on to something more urgent.

"Does he know he has been rescued?" Caleb asked in a tone that showed his frustration. "He does not even connect with us being here," he complained, sure that Asher would not react to his harsher tone.

"He knows he needs to be rescued," she said. "But he is not ready yet. Help him build a fire. Maybe he will connect with you." Marianna spoke eloquently, but sometimes her accent and grammatical errors were obvious.

Caleb turned towards Asher, and he could see that there was not much firewood. He said, "Let me get more wood," and comprehension flickered in Asher's eyes.

Marianna nodded approval, then turned and vanished in the shadows.

Caleb stepped back into the dense woods and gathered sticks to contribute to the fire. When his arms were full, he returned to the campsite.

Asher had taken out a flint and steel and was about to strike it.

Caleb watched with interest, wondering if it would work. He'd tried that once after watching a YouTube video, but after an hour of trying to get a spark to catch, he'd acknowledged defeat and taken out his matches.

Asher had a nest laid out the kindling and had other small wood ready—including the fuzz stick. With one strike, he placed a spark in the nest's heart. He gently blew until there was smoke and then a small flame. As soon as the flame appeared, he brought in tiny sticks and then the fuzz stick. Within two minutes, the flames burned a foot high. Then, in his first acknowledgement of Caleb, he said, "Good fire."

It *was* a good fire. Perfect for cooking.

Asher took out a cooking pot from his pack, measured in just the right amount of water, brought the liquid to a boil, then poured in the macaroni from the box of macaroni and cheese. Timing the boil on his watch, at precisely the right time, he poured the cheese over the white noodles and stirred them together. Then he took two plates and a large spoon from his pack. He carefully spooned equal amounts of the mixture on the two plates, then handed one of them to Caleb.

Caleb smiled and said, "Thank you."

As Caleb ate, Boo walked past the fire and sat next to Asher, placing his nose on Asher's leg and knee and inviting affection. Asher seemed to be very comfortable being touched by the dog. He placed his hand on Boo's head and rubbed.

Caleb thought, *we are making progress with Asher, finally getting him to recognize what is going on.* He remembered Asher's mother telling him his one advantage in rescuing Asher was the dog. She had said, "Just be his friend and give him time to figure you out."

Time was one thing they did not have. The SAR team was closing in. They were probably already at the lake and would find them and want to bring them home. Light would soon fade. This campsite was a very hard place to find, even with the smoke of a fire going. Caleb imagined they would probably be discovered before dark. He wondered if he should leave Asher and go find the SAR team, but he had learned from Nate that in search-and-rescue, leaving the subject was never the right thing to do.

After he had finished the mac and cheese, which he thought was pretty good, Asher took the plates and washed them off with the water from his large jug. Then he reached into his pack, pulled out a bag, and declared with a loud voice, "Marshmallows!"

Hanging from one tree were two sharp pointed willow sticks, another sign that this was a regular camp site for Asher. He loaded two marshmallows on each of the sticks, then he got a box of graham crackers from his pack and a chocolate bar. He broke the chocolate bar and each of the graham crackers in half, and he laid them out on the log that he had used as a cooking table. Then he handed one stick to Caleb and said, "Smores!"

Caleb knew just what to do. He heated the marshmallow over the fire at the end of the stick until it was soft and browning, but not burned, then placed it between the two halves of the graham crackers with the chocolate in the middle. He let the sweet treat cool for just a few seconds and, when his patience had run out, he sunk his teeth into what many would call the world's best campfire dessert.

Asher was working next to him. His first marshmallow had caught on fire. The flaring orange, burned sugar had been disposed of in the coals. But his second one was perfect. Asher's first bite squeezed out soft marshmallow and melted chocolate over his fingers, but he quickly recovered by taking a second and a third bite to finish it.

"More smores!" they both said at the same time.

This was the first time that Caleb had seen Asher smile. It was awkward, but it was a smile. They repeated the ritual three more times until the graham crackers were gone. The sun was setting now, and Caleb believed that they would camp out that night. They roasted another round of marshmallows, and Asher turned, facing the forest, and said in a loud voice, "Do you want one?"

The elf-like woman with the slight accent had returned. "Sure," she said, as she came out of the shadows and into the light. In a motherly way, she sat on a rock next to Asher and helped him pet Boo.

CHAPTER 15

For the next hour or two, the three sat quietly around the fire. Caleb almost forgot he was on a search mission. At first there was no talk. Just silence, flames and fading light.

"Where are you from?" the visitor finally asked Caleb as the firelight danced across the lower branches of the trees.

There was a long pause, and Caleb said sincerely, "Nowhere."

"Everyone's from somewhere," she said in a quiet voice that invited him to explain.

"I live in a farmhouse in Iowa," Caleb explained. "Not on a farm. In a farmhouse. But I spend summers in Lincoln River with Nate and Marie Garner." Marianna sat up when he mentioned Marie.

Caleb just kept talking. "A couple of years ago, Nate and Boo found me in the wilderness area. I had run away from my crazy aunt and my bully cousin and was trying to get back to Iowa." Caleb laughed because that sounded so stupid now. "I say I am from nowhere because I am. In Iowa, everyone in school has lived there for generations. They know I'll be gone before I get to high school, so it's like I have a contagious terminal disease. In Lincoln, they know my cousin is Billy the bully, and everyone fears him, so they fear me, or they know that I'll only be there for two months and then gone, so I'm not worth the investment."

The fire crackled, and the firelight tickled the underbrush that was thick enough to create the feelings of a sanctuary.

"Where are you from?" Caleb asked Marianna.

"It's a very long story," she said, sounding regretful.

Caleb realized the SAR team could not figure out the location of this secluded campsite, and that they would all likely walk out to the trailhead in the morning. He was comfortable with that because Asher made no indications that he wanted to go home. Perhaps he did not need or want to be rescued after all.

"I've got the time," Caleb said, looking directly at Marianna. She looked like she was in her forties, but it was hard to tell because she was very fit and agile, almost like a cat. Her slight accent added mystery and intrigue to her persona. To fill the silence, Caleb added, "Where do you live now?"

"Here," she said.

"Lincoln River?" Caleb said with surprise.

"No. No. In these mountains. At this lake."

"Year round?" Caleb followed.

"Yes. All year. Even in the winter," Marianna said.

"In the winter, you must get cold and hungry!"

"Yes," she said. "But people help, and I have a good place to stay."

"How did you end up here?" Caleb asked.

Marianna told about living under communism in Bulgaria – how the secret police hunted her father, and how her brother was killed, and how she and her mother joined her father living in the woods. "We had three homes, and we would move between them so that we would not be caught." Then she told about the attempt to immigrate, and how her parents left her with a man who pretended to be a priest. She told about the monastery and the refugee camp, and finally the family in Michigan.

"In Michigan, I got angry with the family who had brought me to America. I am angry with everyone who was not a deprived refugee, who had grown up hungry in the woods of eastern Europe. Every time I left someplace, I needed to leave belongings and trusted people behind, but I took my anger with me. I took it to MIT and promised myself that I would get better grades, better research opportunities, and a better job than those soft Americans who grew up in a house with electricity and running water, and friends, and warmth, and television."

Caleb was silent. He couldn't think of anything to say.

Marianna stared at the fireplace, eyes seeing some place far distant. "My professors tell me I am a genius. But they also tell me I needed counseling. Just to keep them happy, I go to mental health clinic. They say take medication, but could not force me. They wanted me to come in regularly, talk with a counselor, and work in a group. I said *no* over and over. No. I must work. Medication makes me too tired to work. Talk takes too much time."

"Eventually, started working. Same requests would come. They called me brilliant, but no one wanted to work with me. Eventually, I ended up at a place in Denver where the boss just let me do my work. He protected me from my co-workers. Some Sundays, his wife invites me for dinner."

"Did you have any other friends?" Caleb asked.

"I did not need any other friends," Marianna said rather harshly. "Friends will eventually let you down," she said, "Unless they are like Asher." The small woman then took the big autistic man's hand and kissed it, and Asher let her do it without reaction.

"How many years have you been here?" Caleb asked.

"Getting ready for my second winter," she said, adding, "almost died in my first winter. Ran out of food. But Asher and his father bring me supplies almost all summer, so this year much better off."

Asher jumped up, took the food sack from his pack, and handed it to her. She smiled. Caleb was surprised that Asher was listening and hearing every part of the conversation. "She lives in the sand bag palace," Asher blurted.

Caleb was not sure what they meant.

"How did you meet Asher?" Caleb asked.

"He was just there, beside the lake, fishing. We talked. Or rather, I talked. Before long, he introduced me to his father. Both seemed to understand that no matter what, they could tell no one that I was living in the mountains. His dad told me what I already knew, that if I had abandoned a car, the police would want me. If I had fished without a license, the Fish and Game officers would want me. If I had built a permanent shelter or stayed over fourteen days, the Forest Service would want me. And, because I had worked on technologies for the government, perhaps the FBI would want me. So, to avoid anyone in a uniform with any authority, my existence is a secret. I do not exist." She paused. "I really am from nowhere."

"I guess we both are," Caleb said.

"We all are," Marianna retorted.

Then she looked at Asher and asked Caleb, "Do you know his story?"

"No."

Asher looked over, giving Marianna subtle, visual permission to tell his story. Caleb was surprised that Asher seemed so disinterested in the conversation, yet followed every word.

She began: "Asher does not know very much about his first mom and dad. They only had him until he was about 18 months and he was not a normal child. At that point, he went into foster care—which you are lucky to have in America. In Bulgaria, a child like him would have been lucky to be raised by a grandmother or an aunt. But most ended up in overcrowded orphanages and did not get enough affection, school or food. Eventually, he ended up in a state-run institution, one that only had a handful of children. They tried desperately to get him adopted out. One-by-one the other children found homes until Asher was the only one left."

"It was what Americans call *miracle*. This older couple came over from Salt Lake City to Denver. They had agreed to adopt Asher even before they met him. He had records they had read. They knew everything about him, and they still took him. He was six then. That was twenty years ago. They have built their lives around him. These are angels."

"It took three years before they could get him into a school. Teachers said he was just too volatile to be around other children. So, his father started taking him on walks every day. First, around the block. Then around the neighborhood. Eventually, they walked around the state. Every day they walked, hiked, even climbed. That's why he's in such good shape. Once he had a stable situation, regular exercise, and loving parents, he could start some special school programs for kids like him."

Boo was lying in the warm reflections of the fire. Then he sat up, his ears and nose pointing back towards the lake. Marianna stood up. "Someone on the lakeshore," she said.

"How can you know that?" Caleb asked.

"The bird calls and the squirrels make distinct sounds now," she said. "I must go see."

Then, without a flashlight or a sound, she stepped into the dark and was gone. As she did, Asher spoke his first full sentence to Caleb. "She can see in the dark."

CHAPTER 16

In the west, the scorching sun was fading. The sheriff thought the search would have been over by now.

On the trail, the SAR team had followed Caleb and Boo up the trail past the PLS, past the waterfall, and into the meadow. It had taken some time, but they had found Caleb and Boo's footprints and tracked them to the lakeshore. In the soft sand and terrain traps around the lake, they had found three sets of prints. Caleb's, Asher's, and Boo's. They had followed the prints along the lakeshore to where they cut into the dense woods. At that point, they found a fourth set of fresh footprints. Small footprints.

They had all heard the rumors about an elf living near the lake. They assumed this was a campfire story gone viral in the minds of campers in this popular backpacking place. When they radioed their finding to the sheriff, to everyone's surprise, they were told to wait for the National Forest Service Vagrant Extraction Team to arrive and help with the law enforcement aspect of this mission that was growing stranger by the minute.

The SAR volunteers had already done enough waiting that day, but the ranchers, teachers, carpenters, doctors, EMTs, people from all corners of the community stopped and waited for the "professionals" to arrive. And arrive they did.

The members of the Vagrant Extraction Team were dressed like a paramilitary group, with black pants and bullet-proof vests. They carried small caliber automatic weapons, radios with earpieces, and wore helmets instead of hats. These officers most often worked alone as law enforcement in the National Forest. But about once a month they would work together, usually with a SWAT team or the Drug Enforcement Agency, to bust up an illegal marijuana growth, or roust out a meth lab that had been set up in the National Forest. Sometimes the people they arrested were dangerous but, for the SAR volunteers, this group was over the top.

The team leader from SAR called the sheriff on the radio: "I'm really not comfortable with this," the SAR team leader said. In his day job, he was a schoolteacher. "This Caleb kid who is helping with Nate's the dog is one of us. The autistic boy is a victim. We need to rescue them, not confront them."

There was a long comeback from the sheriff, then the team leader continued. "We don't care about this small person who might be with them. Let's keep this in perspective," he said defiantly to the sheriff. "We don't need to go in with this group that looks like a SWAT team."

Privately, the SAR volunteers had discussed the situation when they had converged on the lakeshore. One team member said he knew someone who swore they had seen the Silver Lake Elf cleaning up one of the popular campsites and scavenging for food. Another volunteer said he had heard that the Forest Service was still mad that a stack of empty sandbags that a trail crew had been filling to shore up trail banks in the spring runoff had gone missing. The crew had to return to the trailhead and get more bags to complete their trail preservation project.

"Who steals sandbags?" they all had wondered.

"Up at a wilderness lake?"

"Was it the mystery elf with magical powers?" they joked.

The sheriff agreed with his on-scene commander. "It's overkill," he admitted. "Pardon the use of the word 'kill,' but these guys look like they are ready to kill, and that's just not who we are in search and rescue." Then the sheriff explained to the SAR volunteers how the Chief Ranger from the regional office (he emphasized "office,") was concerned that this person they called the "forth party," might guard a meth lab or marijuana grow, and that this situation might (he emphasized "might") be more dangerous than we think. "My colleague on the Federal side thinks our search subjects might be knowingly or unknowingly mules for the drugs, bringing them off the mountain. After all, they come up from Denver every month in the summer to do this hike." He said "Denver" like it was a foreign country and his voice was not convincing because he could see no evidence this story was true.

When the SAR volunteers pushed back, the sheriff said, "Look, this is out of my hands. I have a federal law enforcement officer who thinks his people need to take the lead, so let's stand down and let them do their jobs."

Each of the SAR team members had their own radio, and most had the volume up so they could hear the conversation with their leader and the sheriff. This made it easier for Marianna to hear everything from the cover of the trees, just sixty feet from where they'd stopped. When the team leader and the sheriff finished, defeated in his appeal, the SAR volunteers groused. This provided the distraction for Marianna to slip away in the shadows of the thick vegetation and head back to camp.

CHAPTER 17

"We must go!" Marianna announced loudly as she stepped into the meager light of the dying fire. Caleb could see that she her hands shook with barely contained fear. "The men in black with guns are coming. The American secret police," she said under her breath. She was clearly emotionally rattled, and Caleb wondered how he could bring her back to feeling safe.

"They are just search and rescue volunteers," he said. "Teachers, and shop owners—"

Marianna interrupted, her eyes boiling. "This is the worst nightmare. These are the forest rangers from hell. A special extraction team. America is no different. I have seen before." She was spiraling into the trauma of her past, evoking the images of the secret police in Bulgaria that had chased her family for years, and finally caught and killed her father.

"How do you know?" Caleb asked, but he could see the worry had translated to Boo and Asher, who were both tuned into Marianna's emotional state.

"I listened while they talk on radio. We have twenty, maybe thirty minutes before the five evil men come into my woods!"

"Where would we go?" Caleb asked, with doubt in his voice. He thought it might be best if he stayed with Asher in place. They had done nothing wrong. In fact, it might be an excellent strategy for all of them to stay in place and let whoever it was find them and sort it out. But fear was driving this conversation. Her fear.

"I have hiding place. They not find us there. Asher has been there with his father."

"The sandbag palace," Asher blurted out.

"We go there now!" Her English was becoming more accented as the stress of the situation boiled over in her heart. "Not far. Then we hide until evil men in black go away. Then we take you and Asher to searchers."

Asher was already dutifully rolling up his sleeping back, but Marianna said, "No time for that. I have what you need in the cliff house." But Asher resisted. He wanted all his camping gear packed in his pack in exactly the same way that he always did.

Caleb was worried. It was all happening too quickly. He had heard Nate talk about speeders running from the police and "always getting caught" in their driveway or at their girlfriend's house. But Marianna's fear was genuine, at least to her. He also reasoned that he was by far the youngest person in this group. They were the adults. Marianna was at least three times his age, and Asher was twice his age. Still, he had to ask Asher, "Are you OK with this?"

Asher nodded affirmative. "My dad wanted to protect her," he said. "But he could not come today because he died. So, I came." Asher spilled out words long overdue, admitting that he knew his father was dead and that he saw Marianna, brought her food and offered to protect her.

Marianna was not paying attention to the revelation. She took a dozen flat pieces of aluminum from her pack. Caleb could see that they were soda cans that had been flattened. She began hanging them like Christmas ornaments on the undergrowth around the campsite. "These will confuse their high-powered flashlights," she said. "They will think we are hiding in the bushes." Then she zipped up the tent. "This will also keep them busy, wondering if we are in the tent." Then she placed the cooking pot on the fire. "This will make them think we will return and they will wait." It was clear Marianna had been on the run and knew how to confuse her potential captors and keep them at bay. "Now, we go!"

Caleb grabbed the small search pack with the bivvy bag strapped to the outside, and followed behind Asher, who was on Marianna's heels. Boo brought up the rear.

"When we are completely away from the light of the fire, we will stop and let our eyes adjust. Then we will not need flashlights to see where we are going," Marianna said, with a sure but nurturing tone in her voice.

So through the forest they plodded: three people and a dog, with Marianna leading the way. Caleb thought Asher would be stressed, but it seemed familiar to him, like a grand adventure.

They wove through the underbrush, paralleling the lakeshore, going further away from the popular camping areas. The forest on the right remained dense, but there were some openings in the foliage on the left. The trail was not worn, but every time they came to a rock or boulder field, Marianna had them walk on the hard stuff so that their footprints could not be followed.

Marianna had been running away her whole life. It started in the forests of Bulgaria, then in the abbey, in the refugee camp, in junior college in America, in MIT, in her jobs, and now in these woods where she had been living for a year and a half. Running was something she knew how to do. She knew how to be inconspicuous, even invisible, when needed. And she knew how to listen for the signs and leave before trouble. She knew how to listen to the forest noises, knew when danger was approaching, knew how to listen to people and understand their intentions. She always had at least two escape routes whenever she settled in.

They gradually circled the lake, but kept a considerable distance from the water so they would not be seen. Then Marianna turned east and headed towards a band of sheer cliffs that framed the east end of the basin. It was the band that was in all the photos of the lake. Caleb could see the ragged, often photographed cliffs above them in the starlight. Another hundred yards, and they came to the base of a boulder field. It looked like a place that would discourage any hiker. For a flat trail hiker, it was too steep to go up. For a rock climber, there were too many loose rocks. Marianna went right up the boulder field, struggling in places with the loose rock. Asher also went up, as if he knew the way, so Caleb followed, wondering how this whole crazy situation was going to work out. *At least the rocks will make it difficult for trackers to see signs of our passing*, he thought.

They were all sucking for air when they had climbed a couple of hundred feet up the boulder field. There was a shelf at the base of the cliffs, invisible to the picture-takers and campers at the lake below. They could look out over the treetops and had an only partially obstructed view of the lake and the entire basin. The view included the lights of the SAR volunteers who had built a small fire on the lakeshore while they waited for the Forest Rangers. Caleb could see their headlamps that circled the fire between the lake water and the dense forest. He could also see five equally spaced lights coming into the basin on the trail. Moving quickly, the lights crossed the open meadow and then followed the lakeshore to the SAR volunteers.

"It's good we can see them from up here," he half whispered to Marianna. "But where do we go from here?" As he said that, he realized that Asher and Boo were not around. "Where did Asher and Boo go?" he said in a low voice, not wanting to alert the search that there were people watching them.

"They are in cliff house," said Marianna. Caleb could not see enough of her face in the dark to know if she was serious, but the others were clearly not visible. "I take you in once we see what they do."

They watched from their unusual perch for another ten minutes. The lights of the fast moving ranger team stayed on as they merged with the SAR volunteers, who were by the fire on the beach. Then the five bright lights broke off, and headed in a single file into the dense woods at the same location where Boo and Caleb had entered, searching for Asher. Direct light was no longer visible, but occasionally they could see a glow in the treetops as the rangers advanced on the camp.

Marianna said, "Let's go inside before bad men hear us."

Caleb was puzzled and Marianna picked up on it right away. "This rock cliff echoes sound," she whispered.

Caleb turned and looked at the rock face, but he could see no opening, no cave. If Marianna was an elf, then she was not a magic elf because the rocks did not part on her command. She just simply stepped around a large flat rock and was no longer visible. Caleb followed.

Behind the split rock was a long, straight corridor with a worn path that needed to be navigated sideways. It was open to the sky, but invisible from the valley. From the lake, it looked like it was part of the cliff, but it was a false cliff. He scooted along the path for about fifty feet, where it opened to a small courtyard. In the courtyard was a cooking fireplace, a table made of pine, and some motor parts laid out on a plastic tarp. The rocks stretched over the courtyard to protect the space from most snow and rain, but there was enough of an opening that the smoke from the fire could drift up and out. From the courtyard, he could go in two directions. The first direction went directly into the cliff and was a dead end. But Caleb could see a ladder and ropes carefully arranged.

"Escape route," Marianna said.

The second direction was walled off by a stack of sandbags. There was an opening with a curtain made from a canvas boat cover that had come off along the highway. The door was low, but for Caleb, who was not yet fully grown, it was just fine.

"Please take shoes off as you enter," Marianna said. Then she flipped on her flashlight and said, "Welcome to the sandbag palace."

CHAPTER 18

It *was* a palace, and it was made from sandbags that defined the room nestled under the rock. A string of LED lights that surrounded the uneven rock ceiling drew attention away from the sandbag walls. The floor had two levels. There was a low place to remove shoes, then a step up to a floor which was covered with patches of spotless rugs, clean carpet scraps, and canvas. In one corner, there was a raised cot with a very worn but clean quilt. And there were pillows and a plastic box for a nightstand. Most of the items looked salvaged from campsites or roadsides, but they had been repaired and were exceptionally clean. On the other side of the room, there was a small table with several books on it and a repaired camping chair. Marianna took the food bag from her pack and removed the contents. Then she placed the contents on a horizontal crack in the one rock wall, which served as a shelf. She was well stocked with enough food for a few months, but not for the whole winter. There were several rows of water bottles, from the gallon size to pints, arranged along one of the uneven walls. They all looked full. In the far corner was enough camping equipment to open a small sporting goods store.

There was a neat stack of batteries, including a small vehicle battery that powered the light string. There was a fan and a vent designed so that light would not be visible from outside. She had a small portable shortwave radio in the corner with a wire antenna running outside the shelter to the cliffs above. When Marianna saw Caleb eying the radio, she said, "I can hear Chinese and Russian stations, and lots of Christian preachers in Spanish. Sometimes I can hear broadcasts in Albanian and my native Bulgarian."

Under her neatly made cot, there were other salvaged and repaired gifts left by littering campers.

A clear plastic box contained bedding and pads. She removed a sleeping bag and two pads and rolled the pads out on the floor. "You can sleep there," she said, motioning to Asher. It was clear this was not the first time he had visited. He knew exactly what to do.

Caleb set his bag down and took out his bivvy bag and rolled it out on the second pad. Then, like Asher, he lay down and tried to settle in.

Boo had tried to come in from the courtyard into the sandbag palace, but Marianna shooed him away. "This is no place for dogs," she scolded.

Boo got the message and settled into a snug corner under a ledge that was littered with engine parts. He was tired too, and it seemed like he cared little where he would rest.

This was not a slumber party. They were all fatigued to where thoughts were strained and words cost too much energy to speak. Caleb and Asher settled into their beds, expecting Marianna to lie down on her cot too, which she did, but only until Asher was asleep. Then she rose and slipped out the curtain and into the courtyard. At first Caleb thought she was taking care of her toilet and needed privacy, but after 10 minutes she had not returned. He saw Asher was asleep and comfortable as a bear in a cave in hibernation, so he quietly crawled out of the bag, pulled back the curtain, and stepped into the courtyard. Out there, he could look up and see a narrow patch of sky. Marianna was sitting in the camp chair at the table. She had a small cooking stove and was boiling water for tea. She pulled another cup off the wall.

"No thank you," Caleb said in a quiet voice.

There was a long pause. Several minutes. Then Caleb said," What do we do now?"

That question said everything. Both knew that the search would continue until Caleb and Asher were found. Both knew that Marianna's safe places would likely be compromised. They were looking for a way out.

Caleb began, "Are you scared?"

"Very much." There was a long pause. Then she said, "When I live in Denver, I have a job. I have apartment. I see doctors and take medication. I have neighbors and coworkers. Neighbors bring Christmas card. Only once a year I see them. If I get sick, no one comes. No one knows me. Everyone has children and no time for me. On weekends, I hike in mountains. Mountains are like warm blanket. Safe for me. But too many people near Denver. So I hike in Wyoming. No people. I come here once. Then I come here second time. I stay. No, go back to Denver. My boss gone, my work bad. I have money in the bank, but no friends."

She continued. "The first winter I come here, I live in tent. Freezing. Some nights I go to valley and sleep in the barn with animals. The farmer does not see. I do not steal, but I take frozen eggs and dead chicken. I need food."

"In spring I find food in forest. I fish. But then I meet people camping. Nice people. They leave me food. I get new sleeping bag. I get shovel and ax. Then I find this hiding place. Perfect for me. No one to see me. I can see them from high. Looking down. Very nice. I find the sandbags on the trail and take what I need to build the palace. It is cozy warm. Never hot, never cold. This winter, I am ready."

"But you are alone," Caleb said. "You are what we call 'homeless.'"

"I like alone, and I have a home. These mountains are home. When I have no medicine, then alone is good. Mountains are good. This like heaven to me."

"But Asher will miss you if you stay in this place. And with his father gone…" He did not have to finish.

Marianna said, "Asher not leave me here. I go down with Asher and help him find his mother. His mother knows me."

"And I can't leave Asher either," Caleb said.

"I guess we are like glue," said Marianna. It was the first time Caleb had seen her smile. "Stick together." She put her hands palm to palm and held them.

"Ok," said Caleb. "Let's rest tonight. But in the morning, we need to somehow get off this mountain and get that boy reconnected with his family."

"Ok. You sleep. I watch." Marianna took a pair of binoculars off a hook on the rock wall and placed them around her neck. Then she stealthily slipped out the rock entrance to the hiding place and took a position behind a rock at the base of the cliffs, where she could see the valley and watch the various intruders. Boo quietly stood up, stretched, then followed her out the door.

Caleb watched her smile for the second time as the dog approached. She had bonded with this loyal animal just as she had bonded with Asher, and now Caleb. For the next three hours she sat perched on a rock, watching the search and rescue volunteers pack up and leave, and watching the lights of the ranger team back at the first campground as they tried to figure out where the trio-plus-dog had gone.

What she did not know, is that they already had. When they had been on the lakeshore, before they had gone into the dense forest, the ranger team had launched a drone with night vision capability to find out where to go in the dense forest. They had found the tent but, because there had been no heat signatures at the camp, they knew no one was in it. When they arrived at the campsite looking for clues, they found enough footprints to give them a direction of travel. There, they had launched the drone again and, in the distance, just before the drone made a forced return because of low batteries, they had seen three people and a dog climbing a scree field to the base of a cliff.

CHAPTER 19

Exhausted, Caleb slept for a few hours on the cave floor between Marianna's cot and Asher. He knew that at some point Marianna had joined them on her cot. Still later, like an affection bandit who needed a fix, Boo had found a place on the crowded floor between Caleb and Asher. It was not a peaceful sleep. He had started the day as a rescuer— a would-be hero. Then he had found Asher and lost him again. He had met a homeless woman who was the size of an elf, and who was masterfully living in the woods. Now, he was a troubled fugitive with her.

Caleb remembered the dad joke about paranoia: "Just because you are paranoid, does not mean I am not out to get you."

Marianna was paranoid. She observed like a hawk and ran like a deer. She could see what was going to happen before it happened, and she was always planning a way out. But he was worried that she was too focused on not getting caught by the rangers, and not thinking about how to get Asher, Boo, and himself back to the command center.

It was still incredibly early when he heard the fire in the courtyard crackle. Then Marianna announced that breakfast was served, and Caleb opened his eyes to find that Asher and Boo had already risen and were about to eat.

He pulled back the curtain to see a scene that looked like most kitchens in America in the morning. The nurturing figure of Marianna was cooking. Asher was hungry, and excited, and waiting to be served.

The attentive dog was hoping to not be forgotten. The only difference between this scene and the one played out at Nate and Marie's every morning was that they were hiding in a secret shelter under a cliff overlooking a lake with a group of forest rangers looking for them. But the oatmeal tasted the same, except it was flavored with dried wild strawberries.

Marianna's meal also included hot chocolate, which had come from the food bag Asher had delivered. As they ate their mush and drank the hot chocolate, Caleb decided it was time to ask the hard question. "What do we do next?"

When there was no answer, he said, "If Asher and I turn ourselves in to the rangers, I don't think they will leave you alone, Marianna." He paused. He had been thinking through these options between periods of sleep. "If we try to get around the rangers, then we can walk down the mountain and turn ourselves into the sheriff. After all, he owes me a favor for finding Asher. I think he will be reasonable, but we will still be under pressure to talk to the Forest Ranger." Then he added, "I'd like to stay here, but the longer we stay, the more searchers will converge and try to find us." Caleb reminded Marianna about his own experience being lost and how hundreds of searchers eventually came to help. "We need to get back quickly before these woods fill up with people and the sky fills up with drones and helicopters, and the sheriff thinks I'm a complete idiot."

Caleb finished his speech, and Marianna paused. At first, Caleb thought she was just considering his proposal, but then she twisted her head and whispered, "Someone is coming." She scurried out of the courtyard and down the entrance, stopping short of exposing herself to the outside. Then she cautiously peeked around the edge of the false cliff and down into the valley. Caleb followed her. He wanted to see what she was seeing. As he got close to her position, she saw him coming and put her finger to her lips.

At the base of the scree field, about 100 yards away, were two men dressed in paramilitary uniforms. They had bullet-proof vests, automatic weapons, helmets, sunglasses, and military style boots. They also had radios on their chest packs with headsets. Caleb could see them talking into their headsets, which meant there were others nearby.

It was one thing to see lights in the valley following you from a distance, but it was a whole other thing to see faceless men with weapons just minutes away from your hiding place. Caleb stepped back into the secluded courtyard with the fear of a trapped animal. Marianna followed.

Standing next to Asher and Boo, he said to Marianna in a hard whisper, "It's just a matter of time before they find us here." He could not hide the panic in his voice.

But Marianna was calmer than he expected. "We will go out the back door, then to the top of the mountain. From there, we can ride from the ridge to the valley and you and Asher can go to the sheriff. I will go to another hiding place."

Before Caleb could ask, "How's this going to work for Boo?" Marianna said, "Come. We need to get some webbing on the dog."

In the back of the courtyard, there was a ladder made of lodgepole pines and lashings that rose about twenty feet to a ledge. Marianna climbed like a monkey up the ladder, then along a steep ledge that had a rope that was anchored to the cliff and had knots every few feet for hand holds. She checked the rope to make sure it would hold weight, then she attached a pulley to the anchor and ran another rope through the pulley, then dropped the end of the rope down to the courtyard. She slid down the ladder to the courtyard. "Boo," she called the dog. "You will not like this." Before Caleb could object, she took climbing webbing that was hanging on the wall and laced it around Boo so he would not slip out of the vest. She took the end of the rope and tied a figure 8 knot. Then she produced a carabiner and attached the carabiner to Boo's vest, connecting him to the rope.

"Asher, follow me," she said with confidence. "Caleb, stay with the dog. He will go last."

Once again, she climbed the ladder, but this time slowly, as Asher followed reluctantly. He trusted Marianna, but did not trust himself, and he had difficulty wherever gravity was involved. But as he climbed, he gained confidence. By the time he got to the ledge, he looked like a young boy who had just learned how to climb trees.

"Now, transfer your weight to the ledge and hold on to the hand line," she cautioned. "It will lead you up and out." The two climbers transferred from the ladder to the ledge, then up the rock shelf and out of sight. It seemed like forever before Marianna came scurrying down the rope, then the ladder, landing just in front of the waiting dog. "You're next, puppy," she said with confidence.

Marianna then checked all the webbing and said, "We will pulley him on the ledge, then I will lead him up the ledge and over the cliff. You work the rope, then wait until he is on the ledge and follow. Don't get close or crowd. No room for two people and a dog."

Caleb was not given a chance to object. And his only other alternative was to face what looked like a SWAT team about to knock at their door.

Marianna scrambled up the ladder and onto the ledge. Then she called out to Caleb, "Now pull the rope."

Caleb pulled the rope that tightened around the pulley, then tensioned Boo's waist. To his surprise, Boo's paws lifted off the ground and into the air. Caleb expected Boo would be afraid or panic or bark. But he did not. Then he remembered that Nate had hoisted Boo into a helicopter once and up steep cliffs several times during other searches. His vest was made to hoist. Still, it was strange to see this majestic dog dangling and twisting from a rope. When Boo reached the ledge, Marianna pulled him onto the rock footing and then unclipped the carabiner. Clearly Boo was uncomfortable being at that height. "He looks like a dog trying to do a cat's job," Caleb thought. But he seemed to know what to do as he followed Marianna up the ledge and around the corner.

Caleb scrambled to the top of the ladder, then pulled it up. Using all his strength, he hoisted the top rung, then the second and third, until the ladder was on the shelf with him. Using the hand line, he pulled himself up the steep part. Higher up, the ledge opened up to the valley, and he could see the lake, and below, the entrance to Marianna's hide out. And he could see five men dressed in black climbing up the scree field. If he could see them, then it was only a matter of time before they saw him. As he pulled himself over the rock and out of sight, he distinctly heard one man below cry out, "Look! Up there."

Marianna heard it too, adding urgency to an already urgent matter. Now that they were at the top of the cliffs, Caleb could see that they only had a short distance to get to the top of the ridge.

"If we get to the ridge and follow the ridge to the chief point, then I have an escape vehicle," Marianna said.

Caleb imagined that once over the ridge they would be in another valley and that there would be a road and a car to take them around and back to the trailhead, at that point Marianna could drive away and Caleb and Asher could walk into the command center with Boo.

But when they topped the ridge, Asher could see no road to the new valley below. "Where is the road?" he asked. "And the car?"

"No road. No car," said Marianna. "ATV."

Caleb wanted to ask how she had gotten an all-terrain vehicle this far up the mountains with no road, but he was too busy following Marianna, stepping over deadfall, and busting through brush, trying to get away from the pursuers. He sensed the rangers were right behind them, having found another way up or around the cliffs.

Over the ridge, just below the ridgeline, they came to a strange clearing on the valley side of the ridge. Instead of going down, Marianna went up. It was a stripe that went from the peak of the ridge to the valley floor, and it was relatively clear of trees and debris. He had seen top-to-bottom trails like this before. Nate called them drag trails. These were places where the early settlers and pioneers had climbed up to the high country to get gigantic trees, then dragged them straight down the mountain with mules, or sometimes manpower. Dragging trees had displaced the topsoil, and now, a hundred and fifty years later, trees and brush still had a hard time growing on these strips. Of course, modern machines had helped too. Dirt bikes, ATVs, and even snow mobiles had taken advantage of the sparse enforcement of the Forest Service, and tested their machines on these steep climbs. Often these adventures in high marking the mountain led to rollovers, wrecks, and broken bones. Nate said the mechanized forest was now the bread and butter of search and rescue.

I hope she doesn't think this *is our escape route,* he thought to himself.

Then he heard a voice behind him close enough for him to hear every word. "Hey, they are going up the drag trail!"

PART III
AROUND THE MOUNTAIN

CHAPTER 20

In the last 100 feet from the top of the ridge, the three people plus dog climbed directly up the drag trail. It was the fastest way to the top, and behind them they could see a steep and bumpy, but direct, shot to the valley floor. At the top of the ridge, there was a clump of bushes near the edge with a camouflage tarp covering a small vehicle. Marianna proudly pulled a few cut branches and the tarp off to reveal her bucket of bolts of creation.

Nothing gave Caleb confidence that these four wheels would provide an escape. The ragged collection of parts was a well-crafted piece of junk. It was a piece of art, not a functional machine!

He looked dubiously at Marianna and said, "How do you start it up?"

"Oh, there is no engine," she said, removing any doubt that this was a good idea. "Gravity will give us what we need," she defended. Then added proudly, "I built this myself."

"No kidding," Caleb said sarcastically.

In the last ten years, ATVs had proliferated on the trails around the lake and above the valley. In some places, they were allowed by the National Forest Service if they kept on the trails. But in most places, and this included the lake area and the drag trail, they were not. Yet Caleb had often encountered the machines in places closed to motorized vehicles. He thought no one enforced the law. He also knew that many of the rescue calls that Nate went out on in search and rescue involved careless driving of an ATV. Nate had described the injuries and even death that had come with the illusion of invulnerability and reckless speeds that came with those machines.

The ATV wrecks in the summer and the snowmobile wrecks in the winter were trashing up the forest, leaving tools, spare tires, oil, and parts behind. This was how Marianna had stripped the parts and field-engineered her escape vehicle. It didn't have an engine, but Marianna said it did not need one. From a distance it looked like it would fall apart after rolling ten feet, but Caleb could see that the handy work of this brilliant woman was solid. The tires did not match, but they were all the same size. He could see the steering wheel had clearly come off a car and been cut down to size to fit. The roll bar was so oversized it looked like it came off a tank. All essential systems were in place, even though the cosmetic appeal had been ignored. It looked like junk, so it would tempt no one who had or would come across this empty machine hidden in the bushes at the top of the old drag trail.

"It only holds two of us," Caleb skeptically pointed out.

"You ride in the back. I drive," Marianna said. "Asher, sit next to me." Before Caleb could object, or come up with an alternative, he heard the searchers in the trees below closing in on their position. They were just minutes away. He looked at Marianna and said, "OK. Let's do it."

"You push behind," Marianna said. "Then hop on quickly because we are going fast." Then she handed him a helmet. It was scraped and battered with a broken face shield. The chin strap was missing, but Marianna had improvised a string tie.

"You need this," she warned. "It keeps the head from being smashed." She patted her head with her open palm.

Caleb nodded.

She put on her helmet, which was a modified climbing helmet, then strapped on Asher's helmet, which was a snowmobile helmet that covered his entire head and made him look like an astronaut. Then she put on a pair of gloves and plopped into the driver's seat, buckling her seatbelt and helping Asher with his. They could hear the rangers just below them, now coming up the trail, not ready for the surprise that was about to blast by.

Marianna looked at Asher and then at Caleb, and gave the signal. Asher clutched the bar on the dashboard and closed his eyes, while Caleb kicked the log out from in front of the vehicle. Expecting to push, he took a step back towards the rear, but the ATV was already moving. It was all he could do to pull himself up onto the back of the vehicle, counterbalancing his weight with the two inside the cab, and hold on for the wildest ride of his life.

At first, he thought he could stand in the cargo bed behind the ATV cab, with his hands on the roll bar, and face whatever was coming. But he quickly realized that even with the helmet on, without protecting the windshield, he would get whipped every time they passed an out-grown tree branch. So he awkwardly sat sideways in the small bed of the vehicle. There, he could twist one way and see through the small window into the cab and get a distorted view of the upcoming ride. He could also twist the other way and see behind. As the vehicle picked up speed, he could see a worried Boo trying to follow them without getting too close to this strange four wheeled monster that was carrying his human friends.

For Caleb, it was a carnival ride flashback. And he did *not* like carnival rides. He felt like he had jumped on the roller coaster ride at the last minute, with no ability to strap in and no sense of what was coming. There was a slow acceleration, but soon the ride was moving too fast to get off. All he could do was hold on.

Caleb felt the nose of the vehicle drop and saw the wheels spin. At first, it was jerked slower by the grass under the carriage and the branches that whipped around the front. But within seconds, it was going too fast for any force other than a wall to slow it down. Caleb hoped Marianna would be conservative with the speed. He did not want to see Asher scared, but he especially did not want to get thrown off at that speed.

The combination of the absent engine sounds and the dramatic speed of the escape wagon seemed like a violation of the laws of physics.

Only the rattling of loose parts warned the oncoming ranger team that this ground rocket with wheels was coming their direction. Caleb looked out the front window to see two searchers throw themselves into the underbrush as the vehicle blew by.

"I think that's them!" one of the ranger team proclaimed into his radio headset as the vehicle bounced down the mountain. Caleb turned around to see the ranger roll over in the grass, scattering his gear across a wide area. The ranger recovered after the vehicle passed. He stood up, looked directly at Caleb, and uttered some words that Caleb could not say without being put in time-out by his parents. As they disappeared over the next little ridge, Caleb waved at the fully armed man dressed in black and smiled. He knew he would not be recognized inside the helmet. Then he renewed his grip and hung on for dear life.

His renewed grip came just in time. The vehicle launched off a rock, flew over a log, and landed hard, knocking the wind out of the boy. Before he could recover, a second bump over who knows what sent Caleb two or three feet into the air. Had he not been holding on extra tight, he would have landed in the dust on the rocky trail in the rear-view mirror of this vehicle that had no mirrors. As it was, he guided himself back into the bed of the ATV just in time to hear Marianna say, "Are you still with us back there?"

She did not have time to listen to his answer. With the skill of a NASCAR driver, she wove the vehicle between boulders and trees. The trail leveled out for a bit and, as the vehicle slowed, Caleb could see Asher open one eye. *Brave*, he thought. *Brave Asher.* As the one eye opened, the second followed, and the vehicle rolled more slowly, like the rollercoaster just before a big drop. Asher could see what was coming, and Caleb heard a deep guttural sound coming from Asher's chest.

As the nose of the vehicle dropped for the second time, Asher's groan turned into a low-pitched scream. Not a scream of fear, but a scream of joy. Asher threw his hands up, hitting the top of the cabin. He looked like one of those rollercoaster riders who deliberately ride in the front row in the first car. He was smiling ear-to-ear, screaming, and full of joy.

The next section of the trail was smooth and fast. It seemed twice as fast as the previous section, because there were no bumps. Caleb glanced through the front windshield and saw where the regular trail cut across the drag trail. There was a barrier built by forest rangers to prevent ATVs from using the drag trail, and a pile of dirt to block access. The vehicle hit the back side of the berm, blasted through the signage, and launched airborne.

If this had been a movie, the vehicle would suddenly have moved into slow motion as the camera emphasized the smooth sailing through the air. But it was not in slow motion. The vehicle cleared the cutting trail in less than a second and smashed into the ground on the other side. Clearly front-heavy, the rear wheels left the ground as it rolled on its nose. Expert driving, luck, and gravity sent Caleb slamming back down in the back bed of the ATV and kept the vehicle from flipping over nose first. Caleb was sprawled in the back, bruises forming on his butt and back. But so far there were no serious injuries, at least that he knew about. He could see that they were more than halfway down the hill. Caleb assumed they were traveling between forty and fifty miles per hour, though it might as well have been a hundred miles an hour. He could also see that another, bigger launch was coming.

This time they were in the air longer than Caleb ever thought a vehicle without wings could stay in flight. As they drifted sideways, he wondered if the vehicle had shown up on the air traffic radar, or extended above the treetops. But when they dropped, they did not hit hard. This time, the landing conformed to the angle of the fall, then gently contacted the ground.

But the smooth ride did not last long. There was a log across the road. Not a big one, but big enough to cause trouble. Caleb instinctively stood up and leaned back. With the new weight distribution and the lack of engine weight, the front tires lifted off the ground just in time to hit the log halfway up. The ATV bounced again, and this time Caleb's legs hit the ground just as the ATV slowed. He grabbed the tailgate and was dragged for ten or fifteen feet, then he pulled himself off the ground and back into the ATV bed just in time for another slam.

This time it was not as severe, but the machine was at its limit. One of the back wheels wobbled. It was no longer true. The front windshield was cracked, and Caleb noticed that Asher's door had been torn off.

No longer in the gigantic trees, Caleb could not see a need for such speed. He tried to temper his voice, but his fear and frustration came roaring out. "Slow down!" he yelled. "They can't be following us." Even though he could see Asher was having fun, Caleb'd had enough. "Slow down!" he repeated.

Marianna did not take her eyes off the trail or her hands off the wheel. She stomped on the brake petal and pulled on the parking brake to no effect. Then she yelled into the windshield, "No brakes!"

It took Caleb a few seconds to process what he had heard. She was driving without brakes. She had been driving the entire time without brakes. They were at the complete mercy of gravity.

Now rumbling through the brush, Caleb wondered how they would stop. They were, perhaps, a half mile from where the forest ended and the farms began. He could see about two hundred feet ahead, and then another drop. Maybe he could stop the ATV by dragging his feet before the next big down. Bad idea. The second he placed his foot near the ground, it was slammed by a rock and his leg folded back. He would not be trying that again. They were trapped on the roller coaster, and the track was about to end.

Up and over the last ridge they went, and Caleb could see the stream below them. On the mountain, it had been a small stream, the kind you could jump across. But below them, it had pooled in the rocks. There was only one narrow way between the boulders to the gravel on the other side. They were moving too quickly for words, so he leaned out over the cab and pointed. Marianna had already seen it. They dropped the smooth trail, then rattled across the gravel flat, and splashed into the water. The pooled water slowed the vehicle, but it clearly had enough weight and momentum to keep traction on the stream floor and send a plume of water cascading above them. Just as hoped,

Marianna slalomed the four-wheeled vehicle, wobbling wheel and all, between two rocks, then made a sliding turn around another. The ATV bounced over the small rocks, onto more gravel, then up the other side of the stream, slowing considerably—almost to where Caleb thought he could get out.

"It's almost over," he said to himself, waiting for the full stop to come before he rolled his bruised body out of the back of the vehicle.

But it was not over. Just as he was ready to relax, the nose dropped again, and the ATV picked up speed. The rattling sound of bits and pieces shaking against one another built to a roar. Caleb was amazed that it had held together, that the wobbling right rear wheel had not come off.

"Hold on," Marianna announced as they crashed through a long pole fence with a sign that said, "Private Property." This fence marked the boundary between the forest and the farm, government, and private land. Caleb also hoped it marked the end of the ride.

The collision with the fence shattered the windshield and ripped the hood of the front of the ATV. Caleb also noticed that Marianna's door was now missing, though that could have happened at the stream crossing or while they were speeding up through the bush. He had scrapes, cuts, and bruises, but no injuries. The mostly demolished cab had protected Asher and Marianna in the crash.

Caleb reached up to take off his helmet, and he realized it was not there. It had been torn off without him noticing.

The good news was that they were in one piece, and most of the forest and steep slopes were behind them. The bad news was that they were still moving. This time on a more gentle slope, but with no rocks, branches, logs, or pools of water to slow them down.

And there were cows.

The cows were pastured in this field of tall grass, and once again they were moving at neck-breaking speed with no brakes. Caleb glanced through the little window, and his eyes widened in shock. The front windshield was spider-webbed to the point of obscurity. Marianna couldn't see.

Caleb called out directions in a slightly hoarse voice. "Slight left. "Right. Right again."

She dodged the animals but did not dodge the cow patties which were now being flung into the air by the wobbling wheels of the ATV. The stink was the least of their worries. Caleb could see another fence coming up fast. With little protection left on the ATV, all three riders leaned sideways as the vehicle crashed through another long log fence. It was a good thing that they did, because the lower rails of the fence quickly gave way, but the upper rail held fast. If they had not ducked, it would have smashed their heads at forty miles per hour.

On the other side of the fence, they encountered closely mown grass. With nothing to slow their roll, it seemed like they would continue down the recently mowed hay field. Caleb did not want to go through another fence, but if they did, they would be on a road, and perhaps they would roll all the way to Lincoln River. He glanced over the cab and could see that Marianna had a plan. She was headed right towards —

Everything went dark. Caleb could hear Asher laughing his strange laugh, and Marianna making a spitting sound as she tried to clear her breathing passages. The impact had separated Caleb from the vehicle and he was surrounded by soft and it was dark. He relaxed and felt the pain from his bumps and bruises that told him he was not dead. Just as he got comfortable, the light opened up above him and he saw the face of an older man wearing a straw hat and blue, worn coveralls. The old fella was pushing the hay away as he said in a laughing voice, "Wow, you kids sure made a mess of my haystack."

Stunned, Caleb grabbed the reaching hand of the smiling farmer, who pulled him to his feet. "I think we wrecked your fence too," Caleb said.

The farmer laughed again. "All that can be repaired. I'm just glad you are OK. Haven't you guys heard of these things called brakes?" the old man said in a friendly tease.

"No brakes," said Caleb, his heart still beating so hard he could feel it in his throat. "We had no brakes."

On the other side of the ruined haystack, there was a trail of hay leading to another smaller hay stack with four wheels. It was no longer moving, but he can hear the two people who felt the urgent need to exit. Marianna was the first to push through the hay driver's side. She brushed hay from her hair and spit out some grass she had inhaled. Then Asher pushed through.

Caleb expected to see fear and panic. But the autistic boy rolled out of what was left of his ride and onto the hay, voicing a deep, uncontrollable laugh. Caleb was glad he did not know the danger they had just experienced.

"My name is Bill, and that's my wife Kathy coming through the pasture over there in that power chair. Watch out for her," he said with a wry smile. "She's a force of nature."

"That your dog?" the woman in the chair called out. Caleb turned just in time to see Boo come up over the rise and into the field. His tongue was dragging, and his lower body was wet from having crossed the creek. He had done his best to keep up with the escape wagon, but it had just gone too fast for his paws. Boo stopped at the woman in the chair and put his chin on her knee. It was his body language request for love, and the woman knew just what to do. Caleb watched for a few moments, then said, "Yeah. That's my dog."

CHAPTER 21

Their first kiss came three years after graduating high school. She had caught Bill's eye many times, and he'd wondered *what if?*

Kathy McConkie was the perfect small-town girl. She was not the most beautiful, not the smartest, not the most athletic, but she was a perfect package; beautiful enough, smart enough, athletic enough, and always smiling and kind. Even in high school, she knew how to make everyone feel welcome. Bill knew at least two dozen people who said they were her "best" friend, and a bunch of boys who wanted to be her boyfriend.

Bill moved into Lincoln River High in the middle of his junior year. His father had come back to his hometown and family ranch after a string of career train wrecks that had cost him his dignity, self-confidence, and marriage. With his mother missing and his father hurting, Bill had been transplanted into Lincoln River without friends or direction in his life.

To everyone's surprise, Bill could run fast. Not world-class fast, but fast enough to earn a place as a running back on the perennially mediocre Lincoln High football team. He had happened into a senior year when the hopes and expectations of the townspeople were already riding high for a winning season. Bill provided the one element missing from a semi-talented team who was inspired by a brilliant coach to play above their ability.

Kathy and Bill actually met at a school rally for the small school football state championship. He had seen her many times before but had never spoken to her. Both were caught up in the feeling that this was their Super Bowl and, when their brief conversation concluded, she kissed him on the cheek for good luck. He did not wash his face before the game, or for three days after. But this was not their first kiss. It was her kissing him.

Bill scored three touchdowns in a game where his team lost 48 to 56. Small schools just don't have enough decent players to field a defense, so the young men with promise played offense. Baseball players, basketball players, and wrestlers were guilted into playing eight games of humiliation if they at least tried to play defense. "Just slow them down and make them pay for every yard," was the generic locker room speech. But the defensive squad were football players in uniform only.

As with most Wyoming small towns, high school football was a huge deal in Lincoln River. So Bill rode the chance to be almost famous all the way down main street. Everyone who remembered last year's game thought they knew who to look out for. Bill was the unknown kid who surprised opponents with simple end around runs that led to touchdowns. He scored nine touchdowns in his first three games, and the Tag Along Café on Main Street put his picture in the window and promised free pie to patrons if the team went undefeated in season play. Bill and his teammates were the first to celebrate their undefeated season with a pie party in Lincoln River's only café.

So, Bill was a big surprise in high school, and Kathy was a big catch. She was named prom queen, and always told Bill she could not even remember who took her. She ran for student body secretary, beating out one of three rich kids in the entire school who had professionally designed and printed posters and a beauty queen campaign speech. Kathy just got her best friends together, and they stayed up all night making posters. Then, in her speech, she thanked everyone and sat down. She won by a landslide.

After football season, Bill did not have time for much more than helping on the farm and going to school just enough to graduate. To his surprise, a small junior college in Dillon, Montana, offered him an athletic scholarship. When his father found out, he almost burst his buttons with pride. His son was going to college, and someone else was going to pay for it. Bill could not say no, even though the farm needed more labor than even both of them could offer.

High school graduation came and went, and so did Kathy and Bill. Kathy went to the tech school in Casper and became a dental assistant. Bill went to junior college and played football. His heart was not in the game, and his mind was not in the classes. In the middle of his second season, he twisted his knee and spent the rest of the year recovering. Oh, he had done well on the field, but not well enough to get a call from a university coach, so he graduated with his two-year degree and got a job in Rawlings with a trucking firm, first as a driver, and then as a bookkeeper. All the time, he could hear the family ranch calling. At night, he dreamed about the horses running in the dewy meadow, about the cattle roundup, about catching trout in the lake over the mountain, then being home for breakfast with his dad. He wanted to return to Lincoln River, to the place where he might run into the young woman whose smile still followed him around every day, who in high school had kissed him on the cheek before the big game.

The call to return to Lincoln River came sooner than expected. On a Saturday night, word came that Bill's father had rolled the tractor while doing the spring plow in the alfalfa field. The accident had crushed his leg so badly that it was likely he could not work again. On Sunday morning, Bill called his boss and resigned. Then he left his keys on the kitchen table of his apartment, climbed into his old Ford F-150, and headed home.

The next weeks were hard. Bill visited his father in the Rock Springs Hospital in the evening after working all day on the ranch. They mostly talked about the extensive list of things that needed doing to get ready for the short growing season.

Bill surprised his father. He was a good rancher and a hard worker, and he could get more done in a day than his father, though it seemed like there was always more to do.

On the day that Bill moved his father into the long-term recovery care center in Lincoln River, his dad thanked him by giving him an envelope.

"Aw Dad," he said. "You don't need to pay me."

"It's your graduation present," his father said. But he choked on the last word, and Bill could see he was tearing up. He had never seen tears in his father's eyes before. The envelope held much more than Bill had expected. It was the deed to the ranch and a transfer of the water rights to Bill. Bill sat in his father's little room for an hour, looking out the window angled towards the still snow-capped mountains, trying to regain his composure to say something more than, "thank you." But he could not. When he finally turned around, his father was asleep.

Bill's father had been his only parent for more than half his life. He had come to every football game Bill had ever played. And not only had he gifted him the very future Bill wanted, he was now trusting him to be the fourth generation of his family to steward this land.

In a note left by the bed, Bill said, "The big bedroom is still yours when you are ready to come home."

The next day when he visited again, his father awkwardly said, "Son, I don't think I'll be coming home." Three weeks later, he died in the care center with his face looking towards the mountains.

To everyone's surprise, Bill spoke at his own father's funeral. He wanted to say the things no one else could say about his father. Bill also wrote and published the obituary in the local paper. He wanted his mother to know of his father's death, but he also wanted her to know about his life, and the life he had given Bill. Out of a courtesy, he wanted her to know that her son was now alone on a farm in Wyoming. Even with this new thing called the internet, Bill could not find his mother. No one knew where she was, not even her own siblings.

Loneliness could have washed over him, but Bill was busy with the relentless demands of the ranch. He had been forgotten by his high school friends, who had been taken by the scattering wind that came through town after high school graduation and took them all to faraway places. That's how it is in small towns. There is a line of people, often youth, who can't wait to get out, and another group, mostly young adults, who can't wait to get home.

It was a toothache that finally brought Bill and Kathy together. With no mother in the picture to nag him, Bill had neglected his teeth. When the pain of a cavity took him to the Lincoln River Family Dental Clinic, he found himself in a dental chair, mouth open, staring up at a masked face with beautiful and familiar eyes. He was trying to match the eyes with all the faces in his memory, like one of those three fold children's books where you match the animal head with the body with the legs.

"You don't know who I am," said Kathy in a teasing voice. Bill could feel the warmth of her smile under the covered face.

"No, I'm sorry," he said, adding the voice to his clueless brain.

"I don't do this with every patient," she said. "But here is a reminder." She kissed him on the cheek just like she had in high school, and he knew exactly who she was.

CHAPTER 22

That was also not their first kiss, according to Bill. That came much later. Bill was the quiet, shy cowboy. He could run fast, and ride fast, but everything else was slow. After she prepped him for the dentist and assisted the dentist in filling the cavity, the doctor left the two young people in the room for a long time while he did paperwork, hoping that sparks would fly. They flew, but it took a while for them to turn to flame. A few weeks later, after she put a note in the bill the dentist had sent out, they met at the Tag Along Diner at 11 a.m., when Tag (yes, that is his name), took his daily pie out of the oven. If you arrived right at 11 AM, you could have fresh apple or peach pie covered in melting ice cream.

Bill usually had done a day's work by noon, but he was distracted enough to sleep in on this day. He showered and even combed his hair. Then he arrived thirty minutes early and waited. The pie was great, but they stayed through lunch and into the afternoon. More than her smile was magnetic. Everything was. She was someone he could talk to. Someone who could understand him. They talked about how many of their classmates from high school had moved away. For some, the move had launched them into education and opportunity. For others, they wandered, and wondered if they would be welcomed home to the place of their youth. Bill had a tractor to fix, fields to plow, a calving sow, and a dozen other things he had to do, but he had no desire to cut short their time at the Tag Along.

Kathy told Bill that she went to church every Sunday. Bill said, "Do you want me to come?"

"Sure," she said. And he did. Sunday dinner with her family followed, then a long walk through town. He was falling further behind in farm work, and he was falling for her.

The second date was a movie some weeks later. Cowboy slow. In their later years, as they remembered the moment together, they could not agree on the title of the movie. It did not matter. Both were preoccupied. In the dark, in the almost empty theater, as the forgotten film about a faraway place called New York played across the screen, they had their first kiss, and a few more.

As he walked her home that night she asked about his farm.

"I don't know if I can do it," he said honestly. "It's too much for one person, and I'm falling further and further behind. My father would be ashamed."

"Why don't you get someone to help?" she asked.

"Help is scarce," he said. "I mean, no one wants to work that hard, and I really can't afford a ranch hand."

She stopped walking. Looked him in the eye, and said, "I'd be up for that."

It was the second time they kissed, but this time it meant something more. Much more.

He wanted to get married in a year. She wanted to get married in six months. So they compromised and got married in six weeks. It was just enough time to get the church booked, the invitations out, and plan a honeymoon. Because neither of them had ever traveled much, the decision on where to honeymoon was made for them. Kathy's aunt, who hated Wyoming winters, had a time share in Florida which she gave as a wedding gift. Other friends went in together and paid for the plane tickets. In the end, it did not matter where they went or for how long. Bill wanted to get back to the ranch and Kathy wanted to break in her new home.

After the honeymoon, Kathy continued to work as a dental assistant. It was the only source of cash for their partnership. She poured whatever money that was left over at the end of the frugal month into turning the little farm house into their home. The dining room was a monument to the history of the ranch, with pictures going back to Bill's great grandfather and grandmother. Bill's father was featured on a horse in a large photograph. The hallway was a monument to their own lives. Highschool. Football. Family. Each year, there were more pictures. Each year, the ranch came closer to being in the black.

Bill managed the herd well, ran the hay farm, and fixed the machinery. He also had a small cornfield, an orchard, and a massive garden. Kathy helped in the garden and preserved vegetables and the fruit when in season. They also killed a cow every year to keep meat in the freezer and raised chickens for eggs.

Of course, cash was scarce. When they had it, they would fill up the gas tank on the pickup, the ATV, and the tractor. A ranch like this was hard to run without gas. On special occasions, they would get pie at the Tag Along, but never dinner. Too expensive. On Sundays after Church, they would take fishing poles, a frying pan, butter, lemon pepper, and hike straight up the drag trail and over the ridge to the lake. At the lake, they would build a campfire and cast their lines in the water. Usually within the hour they had two or three fat cut-throat trout, or brookies, and they would melt the butter in the frying pan over the fire. Then, they would sprinkle the lemon pepper and fry the fish. On those same trips, if they could see no one else at the lake, they would go for a swim. But the swim never lasted very long because the water was so freezing, even at the peak of summer. Then in the evening they would go up and over the ridge and back to the hard life on this hard land.

In the fall, Bill would sell part of the herd, and after they had paid the feed store and put a little in savings, they might buy a piece of furniture or a new tool. One year, Bill found Kathy looking at a baby crib, and he wondered. But so far, his wonder had just been her wish. One year, when the price for beef was way down, he just broke even at the beef auction. All that work, all those early mornings, and not much to show for it, he complained to Kathy. But in her bright, hopeful voice, she said, "Happily ever after always has a lot of hard work and a few ups and downs." Her words were etched on his heart, and her happiness became his. And they had stayed happy for close to twenty-five years, even though almost everything had changed.

Everything was not the ranch, the relationship, or the routine. Everything was her. Four years after they danced at their wedding, Kathy was hit head on by a twenty-two-year-old drunk driver while coming home from work. The force of the collision and the quick stop sent her hurtling into the collapsing dashboard. Because the old pickup did not have air bags, she slid under the seat belt and was partially crushed by the collapsing truck. Like a switch, the feeling in her legs was turned off. But even with no movement in her legs and a serious head wound, before help arrived, she crawled out of the cab and around to the other vehicle, where she stopped the bleeding on the unconscious driver and saved her life.

Kathy was flown by medical helicopter to Rock Springs, over the ranch, the ridge, and the lake she loved. If she had looked out the window, she would have seen Bill below in the pasture three thousand feet below, mending the fence, wondering why his wife had not yet come home. Then he would look up and see the helicopter and wonder where it was going in such a hurry. Ten minutes later, the sheriff and the minister visited, and Bill's script for happily ever after with Kathy changed.

That was 23 years ago and, in retrospect, both admitted that the course of their lives had not been changed much by Kathy losing the use of her legs. At first, it was hard. There were long days of travel to Rock Springs, but in those days, when he returned to the ranch late at night and behind on work, neighbors and friends had stepped in. Fixed the fences. Painted the barn. Harvested the hay. Even kept the predators from getting after the herd. A cabinet shop in town had created lower wheel chair accessible cabinets so Kathy could work comfortably in the kitchen. A group of neighbors and church members helped Bill install them and remodel the downstairs, turning the dining room into the master bedroom. Then Kathy would not need to go upstairs. From the dining room, Kathy could look out over the whole ranch, and she could see woods, the drag trail, and the sunrise.

Within a year, Kathy learned to drive a special van with special controls. She got very good at rolling out to the driveway on a long ramp, then into her van which she had named "Big Red." During that year, Kathy would go to physical therapy almost every day in "Big Red." But she would stay in town for an hour or two doing who knows what. Bill noticed her late returned, and worried for her safety, but he did not mention this to her. On a Sunday a few weeks before Christmas in the morning church service, to his surprise, Kathy sat at the piano and played "Joy to the World." Bill watched much like a proud parent watching their child. After all the congratulations, Bill cornered his wife. "So, you've been taking piano lessons all this time and haven't told me about it."

"Merry Christmas," she said.

He knew she had always wanted to play the piano, and she admitted she had been spending some of the grocery money on lessons. Later, within a week, Bill quietly sold two of his finest heifers and bought a used piano. "Merry Christmas," he said when the piano was delivered on a snowy Christmas Eve.

At the Christmas service that year, there was another surprise. Just like every Christmas Eve, the regular church goers found many strangers joining for the worship service. With the seats in the small church full, folding chairs were placed along the walls. Bill and Kathy were seated in the front row, where there was a special place for her wheelchair. As Kathy looked over at the visitors lining the wall as the choir sang the first song. She saw a familiar face. It was a young woman, about twenty-six years old now, who had walked in late with a cane, assisted by two attentive older parents. As she slowly sat down, she caught Kathy's eye and froze. The fear clearly visible on her scarred face swept away the melodic strain of the amateurish but angelic choir, which was making their way through "I heard the Bells on Christmas Day." Kathy recognized the face she had not seen since the accident. It was the young girl whose poor decisions had changed them both forever.

The girl twisted and urgently whispered to her parents that she wanted to leave. They could see she was uncomfortable and, not knowing why, resisted long enough for Kathy to launch herself towards the girl. With two flicks of the arms, she rolled her wheelchair right in front of the girl, inches from her face. Before Bill or the girl or her parents could react, as the choir sang, "The wrong shall fail, the right prevail for peace on earth good will towards men," Kathy reached from her chair and took the young woman in her arms, and the two wept together. A place on the wall was cleared for Kathy, and she sat arm in arm with the young girl for the rest of the program.

A few weeks later, Kathy was fitted for a power chair. It had been donated by a generous charity, and it extended her world into the ranch property. Kathy could now get around the garden, the barn, and even out into some fields. The power chair became an extension of her, although a special mechanic had to make modifications so she could get her chair into Big Red. Later, the same charity put a lift in their house, and Kathy could turn the upstairs master bedroom back into sleeping quarters, and the downstairs room with the bay window into her music and sewing room.

So Bill and Kathy continued to have the "happily ever after" they had hoped for, and Kathy's persistent smile was the fire that warmed their home. Every morning, they would take small two-way radios off the charger and place them around their necks. This kept them in touch constantly. Bill worried Kathy might fall out of her chair, which she did twice. Kathy worried Bill might get injured while working. The radios also allowed Kathy to call Bill in for lunch and dinner. Often Bill would come in from the fields to the sound of piano music coming from the parlor, or Wyoming Public Radio coming from the FM dial. In the afternoon, after school on Mondays, Wednesdays, and Fridays, there were piano lessons for school children. Some could pay cash. Others traded goods. Still others just came. The old used piano was the best investment he had ever made.

Two decades into their marriage, there was a long, sleepless night after a final rejection for adoption had been delivered. The car crash had eliminated the chance for biological children, and Kathy had been sure they could adopt. But the social services agency denied her application based on her lack of mobility. It was a devastating blow. But Kathy did not stay down for long. Nieces and nephews, anyone wandering through town without means or a roof over their head, were always invited to stay in the small two-bedroom ranch hand quarters near the barn. When they came, they were well cared for, both physically and emotionally. Kathy knew how to cure the stress that so many carry hidden in their hearts.

To bring in a little cash for the ranch, Bill had trained as a volunteer county fire fighter. A few times a year, more often in the summer, his pager would go off and he would hurry off to a brush fire, kitchen fire, or small out building. Because he lived so far from town, he rarely got to the fire before it was already out. But it was exciting to work with others in the community's service. For his fire service, he was issued a radio. When he was working in the house or on the ranch, he would set the radio on scan mode and listen to all the radio frequencies of all the emergency services.

And so on this sweltering day in the summer, the radio chatter had been going on all day. A body had been found along a trail. Then a boy was missing. But in the early afternoon and evening it got very interesting, much more interesting than a murder mystery on the television. Bill and Kathy listened, first on the search and rescue frequency. The sheriff had Deputy Kanaapu paired with a boy to help handle Nate and Marie's search dog. They were supposed to look for the lost boy, who was now known to be autistic. The deputy could not keep up. Then the boy called in and said he could see the subject. They were soon to be found right near Bill's favorite fishing spot on the lake. But then a quasi-military team came in on the Forest Service frequency. They were all talking in code and pretending everything was urgent and dangerous. By the time it was dark, the SAR volunteers were sent home, and five Forest Service officers took over. They were tracking, reporting, and launching drones. Bill and Kathy listened with excitement as the five specially trained Forest Service rangers tried to track the two boys, the dog, and another unknown person through the dense old-growth trees on the northeast side of the lake.

In the morning, Bill and Kathy heard how they had found the hideout, but the suspects, as they were being described now, had fled just ahead of the rangers. Knowing the geography well, Bill and Kathy got out the game-spotting scope and zoomed in on the ridge. Sure enough, they watched as three people and a dog came into view on the drag trail. But rather than going down, they turned up, climbing to the peak of the ridge. Five crouching rangers, dressed in paramilitary camouflaged clothing, with bullet-proof vests, were right behind. At the top of the slope, one of the three pulled a camo tarp aside and revealed an ATV. He could see them board just minutes before the officers overtook them. From the way it rolled, Bill could tell it had no engine. Gravity powered. Silent. "What a genius," he exclaimed aloud as he watched the three leave five frustrated officers in the dust.

Bill and Kathy watched as the vehicle rolled on the verge of control, descending through the various stages of the trail. At one point, it seemed to go airborne, and Bill said, "I don't think their brakes are working." When they were halfway down the mountain, Bill said to Kathy, "I'd better get out to the upper forty. We're about to have visitors, honey."

CHAPTER 23

Somewhere in the back of his brain during a dreamless sleep, Iawani heard the stabbing sound of his cell phone in his high priority ring tone. Deputy Iawani Kanaapu had been sent home from the search the night before, after he had been ordered down the trail and off the mountain. He was not needed in the command center for the missing boys. The sheriff had tersely told him he should, "Go home and get some rest." It was very difficult to rest when he had disappointed everyone by not being able to keep up with the boy and his dog. He had sent them on ahead, hoping they would return quickly with the lost autistic boy named Asher. But that did not happen. Iawani knew that parents, sheriff, and SAR team volunteers were all disappointed and worried when the search was extended. He could feel the hot whispers of his colleagues in the Lincoln County Sheriff's Department behind his back. And he felt like the sheriff was waiting for the right time to say something to his face. He would be fired, a disgrace not only for him, but for his family.

Now the mid-morning wake-up call after a restless sleep. The screen said it was from the sheriff. Not the lieutenant or the sergeant. But the big guy himself. Iawani took a deep breath. Time to face the music. He cleared his voice, then answered as if he had been up and ready for duty for hours.

"Deputy Kanaapu," he said professionally, expecting the worse and hoping for the best.

"Can you meet me in at the C-Store on the south side of town in ten minutes?" the sheriff said with some urgency.

"Yes, Sir." Before he could ask for details, the sheriff hung up the phone. The C-Store parking lot was a common meeting place for police because it had a large and convenient parking lot, snacks, and coffee. Besides, there were no donut shops in Lincoln River, or in that entire corner of Wyoming.

Iawani moved with lightning speed, pulling on his pants, buttoning his shirt, and lace-up shoes. He wondered if the sheriff was going to buy him a diet Coke to make him feel good, and then lower the boom and fire him. Would he be the first deputy ever fired in the C-Store parking lot? He tried to counter his worries with optimism. He was going to be called back into the search? Or chastised and then put on a desk job. He knew the isolation of a desk job would allow him to keep his dignity but would destroy his spirits.

His shirt was wrinkled and his pants unpressed, but he made it to his car in five minutes, and to the edge of town in three. He wanted to be there before the sheriff to show that he was still a responsible officer who knew how to follow orders and be on time. But when he arrived at the C-Store, the sheriff was already there. His black SUV always looked clear and polished, and his tinted windshield made the vehicle look foreboding, even for Iawani.

He pulled his older model and much less impressive car into the parking lot in the opposite direction of the sheriff's car so that they could talk from their driver's seats by just rolling down the window. The sheriff acknowledged his arrival with the nod of his head and then said, "I'd offer to get you a coffee, but I know you are not a coffee drinker." It was an unexpected personal reference to start to what Iawani thought was going to be a very difficult conversation. With his impatience boiling over, Iawani jumped in. "About yesterday, I'm sorry…"

The sheriff cut him off. "Yesterday was yesterday. Today we need to finish this case, learn what we have learned, and move on." Iawani was puzzled. The sheriff continued. "Now, I know you occasionally visit

Bill and Kathy at the South Side Ranch." Iawani nodded. The sheriff continued, "I used to visit them too when I was working the beat. Kathy makes the best apple pie on the planet, better than the Tag Along Cafe." Iawani nodded.

"I need you to go over to Bill and Kathy's and do a wellness check." The sheriff was speaking in a very deliberate tone. He amplified the words "wellness check."

"What about the search?" Iawani could not help but ask.

"Now listen carefully," the sheriff repeated. "I need you to do a wellness check at Bill and Kathy's. Go in by the north road. Stop briefly at the ranch. Say hello. Make sure they are OK. This is your routine stop, so Kathy will have some pie. Then leave on the south road. Do you understand?"

The deputy said, "Yes." He wondered what was really going on. The sheriff, who was usually direct and to the point, was dodging around like a calf in a rodeo.

"Approach by the north road, leave by the south road. OK?"

"OK."

"When you leave, it is possible, very possible, that you will find one boy and one adult male walking along the south road, as far down as the back door trailhead. They might have a dog with them. A very nice dog. Do you follow?"

Iawani paused. Then said, "You mean…" The sheriff cut him off.

"I don't mean anything. It's just possible, very possible, that there are two missing people who need finding before our over-zealous friends from the Forest Service descend from the ridge and chase them down."

"Then what do I do?" Iawani was seeing his chance at redemption, and he wanted to get things right.

"Well then, you do whatever any good deputy would do, right?" the sheriff said in a mock exasperated tone. "But be sure and put a few miles between you and the ranch before you call it in. I don't want those Feds to have a chance at finding our lost boys."

"Ten-four," Iawani said with a warm smile. "Thanks, boss."

The sheriff smiled back and said, "I hate being called boss."

"I know, boss." Iawani said. There are some things an island boy can do and get away with that no one else can.

Iawani drove quickly, but without lights and siren towards the South Side Ranch. First, the road twisted west around the ridge and foothills that became the mountains around the lake. Then the road headed due south, in a loop through several ranch properties. Iawani took the first one that the sheriff called the north road. After a few miles, the north road turned to gravel and followed the boundary of the National Forest along the foothills. It was the most direct, but not the easiest way to get to Bill and Kathy's ranch.

Every time Iawani went on patrol along that road, he would stop and see the couple who lived in isolation, but who would always invite him in. The sheriff was right. Kathy made the best apple pie in the world, but also peach and cherry in season from fresh fruit coming from their small orchard. Sometimes in the winter, when the homemade pie filling preserves had been used up, she would make chocolate fudge cake with icing made from homemade butter. Or butterscotch pudding made with real cream. He always made time to sit at their table and talk with Kathy. And Kathy always prolonged the visits with "just one more helping…"

As he approached the downturn to the ranch, he found Bill repairing a stretch of fence that paralleled the road and the National Forest boundary. It looked like a vehicle had come across the road and crashed directly into it, but Bill said, "Those darn elk herds," then turned to Iawani and winked. "They don't have many manners."

Iawani got out of his sheriff's car and helped with the fence repair, but Bill scolded him. "I'd like the help, but you don't have time for that. Now run down to the house and pick up the pie that Kathy has ready, then leave." He pointed towards the south road. Whatever the sheriff had staged, Bill was in on it. The deputy got back in his car and followed the driveway to the house. Before he could get out, Kathy was rolling down the ramp in her chair with a warm Tupperware box full of three pieces of pie, then another piece in a smaller box. There were four napkins and four plastic forks. No explanation.

"The small box is for the sheriff," Kathy said. "Now, you three enjoy the pie," she continued, shooing him away like a horsefly. "Be sure and leave by the south road." She could see by his speechlessness that he did not fully understand what was going on, but she did not explain.

Iawani took the containers and said thank-you. Behind Kathy, he could see a set of eyes staring at him from the shadows in the house. "Who is that?" he asked Kathy, who turned around at looked at the windows of her house with a smile.

"Oh, that's our new ranch hand," she said. "Her name is Marianna. Come by and meet her someday, but not today. Now go. GO." She motioned with her hand, and Iawani headed up the driveway, past Bill, who was almost finished repairing the fence, and turned right. As he turned right, he could see in the pasture below the fence repair a large haystack that looked like it was out of place. It looked like it was sitting on top of something and there were tire tracks leading into the haystack. Meanwhile, Bill had finished the fence repair, put up a series of "No Trespassing" signs, and was busy herding about twenty head of cattle into that pasture.

The dutiful deputy followed the south road along the boundary of the forest for three miles as the aroma from the cooling pie slices filled the interior of his car. He drove slowly so he would miss no one walking along the road, but the only thing he saw were a few deer on the Forest Service side, and some livestock on the ranch side of the road. The critters knew to keep the boundary rules, he thought.

Just before the north road looped back to the west, there was a small parking lot near a trailhead. This was the second trailhead to the lake, sometimes called the back door. Few people knew about this trail and even fewer traveled it because it was longer, steeper, and further from town. There were no cars in the parking lot, but right by the entrance was a large young man looking directly at him that Iawani assumed to be Asher. He could see Caleb, but no Boo. Boo was playing in a small stream that paralleled the road for a few hundred feet away. As the car approached, Caleb called the dog, who came to attention and dashed immediately to his side, oblivious to being wet and dirty.

With the dog covered in mud, the first thing the deputy said was, "There is no way that dog is getting into my car." Caleb laughed, but Asher missed the humor in the situation. Then Caleb said, "I can fix that," and he threw a stick in a pool where the water backed up behind the pipe before the stream went under the road. Boo jumped into the water to retrieve the stick without hesitation, then pranced out of the pond, putting the stick on the ground for his shake off, then picking it up again and dropping it at Caleb's feet.

"I guess a wet dog is better than a muddy dog." This time Asher laughed.

The deputy handed the Tupperware container, the forks, and napkins to the two, and they took it. Asher awkwardly said, "Kathy promised pie at breakfast, but it wasn't ready yet." Then he smiled and said, "We got to ride in Big Red with the wheel lady driving." Now Deputy Kanaapu was sure everyone knew the details of the conspiracy except him. They quickly devoured the pie, then piled into the sheriff's vehicle, with Caleb in back behind the prisoner cage with the wet dog and Asher in the front.

Before they had gone twenty-five feet, Asher looked at the Deputy and asked, "Can we turn the red and blue flashing lights on? I like red and blue flashing lights." Iawani flipped the switch. He was pretty sure no one was going to see him driving slowly down the ranch road and back to town with his lights flashing.

Once they were headed back to town on the north loop, Deputy Kanaapu called dispatch.

"1J749 calling 1J100 and all units." There was a pause.

"Go ahead."

"I've found Caleb, Boo, and Asher on the south side of the lake ridge at the trailhead. All parties are in alpha condition, and we are returning to Lincoln River."

"Could you repeat that?" Sally asked. "I think everyone is going to want to hear that." Iawani repeated the message, then waited. Before long, the sheriff chimed in. It was like he was speaking to Iawani but hoping someone else would hear.

"100 to 749."

"Go ahead, sir."

He spoke deliberately, like he was speaking for someone else to overhear. "Let me get this straight. You found the older male named Asher, and the SAR volunteer dog handler named Caleb, and the SAR dog named Boo at the trailhead on the other side of the lake?"

"Yes sir."

"Nice job. Do you think they came down that back door trail?"

"They must have." The rookie deputy could think of no other possibility.

"Ten-four," said the sheriff. "Now, deputy, do you have your go bag?" That was a strange question. Iawani had his go bag for overnight situations in the trunk of his patrol car, but he had never used it. "I'm going to need you to leave immediately to help with a prisoner transfer once you get those boys back."

"Where am I going?" Iawani asked.

"I'll tell you when we meet up at the place where we met this morning."

So, the conspiracy deepens, Iawani thought.

CHAPTER 24

"Damn it." Chief Ranger Rondo McFee slammed down the phone hard enough to make the glass windows shake. "That smug local sheriff has gone too far this time. He looked at the five Forest Service law enforcement officers sitting casually in the chairs around the conference table in his office with neutral expressions that did not hide their apathy. Not caring three weeks after the events in Lincoln River, after they had been mocked by the locals and made fun of in the press, only made the chief ranger more vehement."

"I thought we would finally, after three weeks, get to the bottom of this. But nooo," he said with his voice trailing off.

"He says his deputy found the two boys at the trailhead on the back side of the ridge, three miles from the drag trail. But you say there were tire tracks coming down the drag trail and there were no fresh footprints coming down the back door trail." He motioned to the five. "He says those two boys might have gotten off the trail in places because they might have come down in the dark. You say it was almost 11 AM when they found the two. He says, when I pressed him for details, he did not interview the boys himself. But left that to Deputy Island Boy. What's his name?"

"Deputy Kanaapu," one officer said with dead pan respect.

"Then immediately, before I can interview him, Deputy Kanaapu goes off to Evanston in Uintah County on a prisoner transfer, and he takes three days! Three days to drive two hundred miles. Then when he comes home, he goes on vacation. Back to Hawaii? Surfing? Or Salt Lake? No one in the department knows. The sheriff says he does not track where his personnel go on vacation!" His voice is getting louder, and his officers are looking around, wishing they were in a better place, like stuck on an LA freeway with a flat tire, or in a dental chair getting their teeth drilled.

"I got to interview that Caleb kid at the home of deputy doggy handler…"

"Deputy Nate Garner," the same officer says with respect.

Ignoring the other officer, the head ranger continued. "… And the kid is taking a two-day nap. He's tired because of his ordeal. What ordeal? That's what I want to know. Then, after waiting as long as I can in the Podunk town of the Podunk sheriff, the boy tells me his mom needs to be in the room when we talk because he's a minor. Well, his mom lives in Iowa and apparently spends a lot of time milking cows, or doing whatever they do in Iowa, because she would not call me back."

He continued his exasperated tirade even though he had long ago lost the sympathy his audience. After all, it was these five officers who followed orders and used their highly honed skills on what was now being called a wild goose chase. "Then, I go out to this ranch, looking for the third party. The trespasser."

"The elf," the ranger who was filling in the blanks said soft enough for the others in the room to hear, but not loud enough for the chief ranger to hear.

"The woman who stole US government property, from us…"

"The sandbags," said the officer who was accurately filling in the details.

"That woman in the wheelchair…"

"Kathy McConkie," said the officer. "That woman," the regional director spat her name out with contempt, "would not let me on the ranch property without a search warrant. So, I get the federal prosecutor to go with me to the judge. To a federal court with a federal judge. He says, 'what's the crime?' I tell him about the suspected marijuana grows, or the possibility of a meth lab, and he says, 'any evidence?' I tell him about our history and all the fine work of your officers, and he asks if I have anything more than just someone who overstayed the fourteen-day limit on camping privileges. Then the judge, this Federal judge looks at me and says, 'You expect me to issue a search warrant for the property of a woman in a wheelchair in order to find evidence of a misdemeanor that carries maximum $250 fine as a penalty?'"

Chief Ranger Rondo McFee paused for effect, hoping for sympathy from the obliviously dormant audience. They were all looking forward to being back in the woods or giving out speeding tickets to people driving their ATVs thirty-three miles an hour in a twenty-five miles an hour zone. "Then that judge," he continued, "… that old man, he has the audacity to tell me to find something more important to do with my time." At each paragraph, his voice got higher. Finally, the regional Forest Service director stormed out of the room.

The five Forest Service law enforcement officers looked at each other. The one who had done the talking, who had filled in the blanks for his superior, smiled and said, "I guess we can go, too."

CHAPTER 25

In the two days following the search, Caleb rested in his room. Marie treated him like he was sick and brought him soup. She even set up a monitor in the room and let him play video games. Boo slept on a woven rug at the base of the bed for almost forty-eight hours. The rest period felt like forced isolation to Caleb. There had been a phone call to his father, and a string of visitors at the door. Neighbors and church members brought food and sympathy. A reporter from the local newspaper came but did not get far with Marie.

On the second day, Boo jumped up and barked at a visitor. It was a Forest Service big wig, a short man all dressed up in a green uniform like Smoky-the-Bear. The man, who was not comfortable around Boo, asked Nate if he could talk with Caleb. It did not go well for the pushy man. Nate finally told him he was not to interview Caleb without Caleb's mother present. He gave the man Caleb's mother's phone number in Iowa. Caleb knew his mom was on a one week "yoga" retreat with her friends somewhere in New Mexico. She was not to be disturbed unless there was an emergency. This was not an emergency.

A few days after avoiding the interview with the chief ranger, Asher and his mom came by. Boo greeted Asher like a long-lost friend. "I got a job!" he blurted. "I am a bag specialist and shopping cart technologist at the market. And they are going to pay me money! I'm going to work there every day this summer." Asher bubbled with excitement, and he could not stop talking. "Bill and Kathy wrote a letter to the owner of the market. He hired me on the spot. Bill and Kathy were there on my first day. And guess who was in Big Red when I carried the groceries out?" Asher did not wait for a guess. "Marianna! She's my friend. You are my friend. Now my boss is my friend and so is Marie. All my friends live in Lincoln River, so we are going to live in Lincoln River where my friends are."

Asher's mom said they liked Lincoln River. After the death of her husband and Asher's father, the town embraced them. In fact, they liked it so much that Asher's mom, who was quite wealthy, purchased a small and nicely restored old house in town. They would spend summers in Lincoln River and the school year in Denver, so that Asher could attend a special school.

For the next twenty minutes, Asher talked non-stop about all the townspeople he had met at the grocery store. He seemed to remember every detail about what they were wearing, purchased, and said as he helped them load their groceries. This was more talking than Caleb had ever heard from Asher. Asher was twice Caleb's age, yet they were close friends.

The Dudley-Do-Right of the Forest Service had tried to talk to Asher, too. But his mother had protected him. "We don't want him to relive the trauma of that night," she told the chief ranger, who had said he was just trying to figure things out.

A few days later, Asher's mom took Caleb, Asher, and Boo out to see Bill and Kathy. As they approached the ranch from a distance, Caleb could see the straight drag trail that went from the ridge to the back of the property. He was amazed that anyone had survived that steep drop in a vehicle without brakes. Only the skill of Marianna had kept them upright. At the ranch, Caleb was amazed to see that the once motorless ATV made from abandoned and salvaged parts was parked in the garage. Standing over the hood, covered in engine grease, with rags coming out of the pockets of her coveralls, was Marianna. When she saw the two boys and the dog, she hurried to them with her arms opened. They looped their arms around each other, then pulled Boo into the circle. The three of them stood for a moment in a three-way embrace, with a tail wagging golden retriever in the middle, and said nothing. Bonded for life, there were no words for their feelings.

Marianna was comfortable living in the ranch hand quarters and working for "room and board." There she could live isolated, but also connected and protected. She did not need Bill and Kathy to pay money. Somewhere in a bank account in Denver, she had more money than she would ever need. What she needed was the safe and supporting place they could provide. Kathy put her to work figuring out the special mechanics of her electric wheelchair. Bill had her finishing the rebuild of the ATV. She was riding horses and moving cows, and she even heard Bill and Kathy talking about a vacation. Something he could never have done before without someone to look after the ranch.

After the hoopla about the escape had died down, Bill had gone up to the hiding place on the mountain wearing a hood and a scarf so that the trail cameras posted by the forest service could not recognize him. He had retrieved the engine parts Marianna salvaged; then bought a few more in order to get Marianna what she needed to turn this ATV into a useful piece of machinery for the ranch. But the other reason he had gone to the mountain was to retrieve an old quilt. Handmade, in thick Bulgarian cotton, with frayed corners, patches, and stains. It was the only thing Marianna called home.

A few weeks earlier, before the search warrant had been denied by the federal judge, the chief ranger also tried to see if Marianna was living at the ranch. For two days, he sat in his truck on the gravel road between Forest Service land and the ranch and watched with his game spotting scope every movement on the ranch. He assumed that Bill and Kathy were unaware that he was there. After a second long day in the cab of his official car, he watched Kathy wheelchair out of the farmhouse with something in her lap. She made her way into the garage, then the big red wheelchair ready van emerged, and he assumed she was going to town. She exited the driveway, and she rolled right up to the ranger's SUV. Then she dropped her ramp, and wheeled herself over to the window and presented him with a pie in a container.

"It's apple, grown from those trees over there. I hate to see you up here all by yourself and hungry. Would you like to come to dinner?"

Chief Ranger Rondo McFee was flabbergasted. He politely declined the invitation, and after a few pleasantries, started his engine and withdrew. Three miles down the road, when the smell of the fresh baked pie had permeated every corner of the truck cab, he pulled over and feasted on the best apple pie he had ever tasted.

As Caleb stood there in the barn with his friends, Boo went into an alert position. "This darn chair makes it impossible to sneak up on anyone," Kathy said. This wonderful host looked at Caleb, then each of the others, then held her hand out to the dog. In her presence, they each felt more than safe. They were admired. More confident. More grown up. "The pie will be out of the oven in a few minutes. The sheriff is on his way to join us." She paused, and her voice changed. "I'm sure you all have some questions about an alleged cover up. But when he gets here, let's just enjoy the pie."

The next day, Nate and Marie, Bill and Kathy, Asher and his mom, and Boo made the long drive to the little regional airport that would take Caleb to Denver and then home to Iowa. At the airport, Asher's mom gave his boarding pass to the gate agent, who doubled as luggage manager and ramp attendant. She produced a magic card with platinum status to upgrade Caleb to first class. But the eight-seat regional plane did not have first class, so the benefit did not kick in until Denver.

In Denver, everyone in first class was wearing a suit or a tie exceptCaleb. Below, he could see the flat fields of Colorado, then Nebraska pass under the wing, as the plane rose to cruising altitude. The roads cut the farmland into perfect squares, with buildings ordered at the end of driveways. In this relatively flat world below, everything seemed predictable.

But Caleb's summer had been anything but predictable, especially since meeting Asher and Marianna. In about 60 minutes, he would be back with his parents, back with his normal life in Iowa. While he was in Wyoming for the summer, his father received a research grant. Because of the grant, they could now afford married student housing at the University of Iowa. Caleb was disappointed because he liked the open spaces of the farm they had been living on, even though it meant his father had to drive thirty minutes to work every day. It also meant that he would change schools again, but he was used to that.

If there was one moment Caleb would remember from his finding Asher summer in Lincoln River, it was not his grand adventure searching for his new friend, meeting Marianna, or the roller coaster ride into Bill and Kathy's back pasture. It was not the praise from Nate and Marie for finding Asher, or the kindness of Bill and Kathy, and her ability to build bridges with homemade pie. It would come three weeks later, after all the excitement had died down, and Caleb and Marie were invited to a local day camp for very young children.

"Dogs do more for us than we can see," he told the group of young children in a day camp. "They help us know ourselves, and they bring us together." These were big words for young children. "Now. Do you want to meet Boo?" The energetic crowd affirmed. At the back of the room, Marie released Boo, and, to the delight of the children, the anxious-to-please golden retriever bounded onto the stage and stood at attention next to Caleb.

With Boo looking on, Caleb talked in a big brother tone and told what these children needed to do to not get lost in the woods. The children were distracted by the dog until Caleb began telling his own experience of being lost. One by one, he hooked their attention with the details of his overnights in the wilderness, the Oreos, the straw bed, the storm and how Boo had found him. As the attention in the crowd shifted from Boo back to Caleb, the dog wandered off the stage.

In the front row of the room that doubled as the camp cafeteria, there was a section reserved for those who needed wheelchair access. One small boy in a power chair sat alone in that row, isolated with his attendant. His face showed his fear and courage. He was afraid of being in the unfamiliar space of a summer camp, away from his parents with strangers to care for him. There was a list of daily activities he could not do. But he had the courage to come and be in front of all these children his age and be different. For three days, no one except the attendant talked to him. No one had reached out. He had become like a piece of furniture.

The majestic retriever casually approached the apprehensive boy and sat in an open space a few feet away. He was waiting to be welcomed. After a moment, the boy looked up and made eye contact with the dog. Twisting his head slightly and using his warm brown eyes to draw him in, Boo moved closer once the aura of fear vanished. The boy could not help it. He reached for the dog's inviting ears, ruffled his fur, and stroked his head. Boo then placed his chin on the boy's knee and left it there for the rest of the presentation. The boy in the wheelchair was the envy of everyone in the building.

While everyone saw the dog cross the line, most did not notice the camp counselor, who was his attendant. She had been assigned to this boy for the three days and had tried everything to make him feel welcomed and unafraid. She tried to get others to play with him or do camp crafts. Her efforts fell short, and the boy in the chair mostly watched as the other children hiked, rode horses for the first time, or climbed a ropes course. With the dog drinking in his affection, the boy in the chair broke into a broad smile, and the sixteen-year-old first year camp counselor could not keep back her tears. Caleb saw it. The moment said everything. He watched Boo rescue another person.

ABOUT THE AUTHOR

Scott Hammond tells stories of resilience that are inspired by his experience finding lost people with his search dog "Boo." He is a committed teacher (Utah State University), an award-winning author, a speaker, and is regularly heard on radio and podcasts nationally. He is also a member of one of the best search and rescue teams in the United States where he participates in about 50 rescue missions a year.

"An engaging and powerful story of a rising spirit,
a courageous dog, and the lights that lead us home."
–Richard Paul Evans, #1 New York Times bestselling author of the Michael Vey Series
SCOTT HAMMOND
FINDING
CALEB
SEARCH AND RESCUE DOG SERIES | BOOK ONE

NOTE FROM SCOTT HAMMOND

Word-of-mouth is crucial for any author to succeed. If you enjoyed *Finding Asher*, please leave a review online—anywhere you are able. Even if it's just a sentence or two. It would make all the difference and would be very much appreciated.

Thanks!
Scott Hammond

We hope you enjoyed reading this title from:

BLACK ROSE
writing™

www.blackrosewriting.com

Subscribe to our mailing list – *The Rosevine* – and receive **FREE** books, daily deals, and stay current with news about upcoming releases and our hottest authors.
Scan the QR code below to sign up.

Already a subscriber? Please accept a sincere thank you for being a fan of Black Rose Writing authors.

View other Black Rose Writing titles at
www.blackrosewriting.com/books and use promo code
PRINT to receive a **20% discount** when purchasing.